Printed in the United States of America

First Printing, 2016

ISBN -13 : **978-0-9977987-0-8 Paperback**

Mother II Son Publishing LLC.

Designed by Richard E. Sabree-Feimster

www.facebook.com/MOTHERIISONPUBLISHING

EMAIL: MOTHER2SONLLC@GMAIL.COM

P.O. BOX 8576, NEWARK,NJ 07108

Acknowledgements

First, I want to thank the good Lord God almighty for carrying me every step of the way. Without him nothing would be possible and with him anything is possible.

I want to thank my Son and Daughter, Richard and Giovanni . They have been with me through this journey from day one when I spoke it into existence and they believed in me ever since. There were times when I would fall short and put the pen down they served as a constant reminder of why I couldn't just let the ink dry.

Richard we laughed and we joked and we talked for hours on end. We stuck together even when times were hard. We shared ideas and turned them into a reality. . You put in hard work and dedication, exploring your creative talents and you helped bring this dream to real life. There is so much that we have learned through this journey and will continue to learn because this is only the beginning. Thank you

Giovanni you sat and listened even when you were tired from a long day at work. We sat up early mornings and late nights while you shared your thoughts and ideas .You helped me build and you were one of my biggest fans. Thank you for believing and supporting me.

Ursula My best friend. I had the left hand and you had the right. You went in the cave with me and you made sure things were going the way it was supposed to. You sweated it out with me all the way to the finished project. Thank you for being my friend, my best friend. You've been a huge support and there was no way you were gonna let me fall short.

Doreen – My Sister from another mother. I knew you always believed in me from day one. You saw the vision the same way I did. At times it's like you saw it more than I did. You were ready to see this go into effect right away, and I had to say to you so many times I'm not ready. But you kept pushing me and you brought the characters to life so much I started believing they were real (laughing to myself). In you're mind you already put the book on the big screen before it even went into print ha-ha! You've been ready.

To My baby sister Trimaine, thank you for believing in me and sharing your ideas and supporting me. Sitting on the phone listening to me while I would read what I would write to you over and over again. Thank you for your support during the photo shoot.

I want to thank My Baby Sister Quinn, my Sister Joanne, my big Sister Darlene.

I want to thank Uncle Herman and Uncle Melvin. And thank you to a special someone in my life Ibrahim for believing in me and supporting me. I want to thank my nieces Triseama, Marquee Julius, Toney and. I want to thank everyone else for their love and support in making the dream happen.

PROLOGUE

Sprawled out on the cold marble bathroom floor after a long night of drinking and drugging, Mahogany crawls to her knees feeling her way around the dimly lit bathroom slumping her head over the porcelain toilet, hugging it tight while vomiting chunks of undigested food from the night before. Feeling miserable trying to decipher the cause of her sudden illness, she thought to herself.

"Damn I have to lay off that E&J or shit I promised myself that I was gonna stop ordering from that rat hole Wong's since the last time I got sick after eating the egg foo young. Or shit face it girl, you probably got a hold of some bad shit I have to stop snorting that poison through these pretty little nostrils of mines."

She slowly stands to her feet. She stares back at her tainted reflection in the mirror through the ruptured blood vessels in her eyes after violently throwing up chunks of food which turned to pure bile then dry heaving once she emptied her stomach of last night's dinner. Her hair is matted down on one side, and the rest is just wildly standing on the top of her head. She has sleep lines imbedded in her left cheek from the swirls on the marble flooring. She leans over the washbasin turning on the cold water drenching her entire face.

The Phone rings and it's her best friend Veronica. Veronica had just returned from a two week vacation in Cancun. She had been trying to reach Mahogany the night before and she was starting to get worried.

"Hello."

"And hello to you to. I have been trying to reach you all night. Where the heck you been?"

"Oh girls please, take it down a few notches. My head is still in a spin and my stomach feels like there's a burning hole inside."

"Well what's going on with you girl? "

"Trevor had a party last night and well, you know, the rest is history."

"So let me guess, you was drinking for one and was you getting high as well?"

"Yes and yes."

"Damn before I left town you said you was gonna lay off that. Come on girl you promised. I mean we all swig a drink or two, maybe even three or four but you know you don't have to partake in that other crap. You're bringing yourself down each and every time and you know it. But hey we talked about this already I'm gonna leave it alone. It's no wonder why I kept having these weird dreams and worrying about your ass."

"Listen, can we talk about this later? Cause right now it sounds like you talking to me through a bull horn or something."

"You know what have it your way. You and that damn Trevor!"

Click!

Veronica hangs up the phone. Mahogany is standing there with an expression like a child who has just been scolded by a parent. She looks around the house and it's a complete mess. Empty beer cans and bottles of liquor all over the place, empty food cartons, and ash trays filled to the rim with dirty cigarette butts Trevor lying across the bed fully clothed including his shoes and his feet hanging off the bed.

He is snoring so loud it sounds like a bear in hibernation. His cousin Jean is stretched out on the living room sofa reeking of alcohol. Much to Mahogany's surprise, she noticed the front door was never locked. She gets pissed off but she's not even sure who the last person was to leave her house.

She couldn't be upset at nobody but herself because she allowed herself to even get to that level. She fixed herself a cup of coffee, something she referred to as muscle juice and commenced to cleaning the disgusting mess. Once she was done power cleaning she decided to take a bubble bath and clear her head. She slowly began to feel like herself.

She decided to give Veronica a call back.

"Hey Veronica."

"Well well well, look what the dead has risen, how you feeling?"

"I'm feeling better."

"That's good. What about Trevor, did he get sick to?"

"No he's good."

"Well you tell Trevor that I said."

Mahogany cuts her off.

"Hold that thought. Whatever you want to relay to Trevor gonna have to be when he comes out of hibernation."

"Oh yeah y'all was partying hard last night."

"Party or not you should know. Trevor is just like a bear. He won't eat drink or even get up to take a piss most of the time when he is like that. All he need is air and he can do this as long as I allow it to go on. That husband of mines is a mess."

"That's a damn shame. So anyway tell me, what do you think made you so sick in the first place? I mean you are a seasoned vet with your shit so I find it a bit strange. You seemed to be going thru this whole stomach thing quite often though even without drinking or whatever."

"Girl I can't call it I mean this time was crazy. I was throwing up some yellow and green mess and at one point there was absolutely nothing left but my body kept going through the motions I was just gagging."

"Oh that's serious; no wonder you sound so hoarse. You were tearing up the lining in your stomach and that green and yellow mess, as you call it, that's Bile."

"Bile? What the hell is that?"

"A well research show that Bile is a fluid that is made and released by the liver and it's stored in the gallbladder. The ghetto explanation is girl you tore out the lining of your stomach." Veronica says while laughing.

"Veronica that shit aint funny; it sounds very serious to me. Why did that happen to me?"

"Well most of the times Bile is a result of food poisoning, or alcohol poisoning. You know if you drank too much and if you let me tell it also when a woman is pregnant."

"Now I can understand the food or alcohol thing but Pregnant? Child please."

"Child please my ass! It's not impossible. The past month you and Trevor been going at it like rabbits you said it yourself."

"You funny."

"Aint a damn thing funny girl, I been dreaming of fish and water and you know what the old folks say about that. Not only that think about how you been getting sick out of the blue lately and that's even when you haven't done anything extra."

"Girl it could be a combination of things, from drinking too much, or food poisoning."

"Okay, you are in denial for some reason. You been drinking the same shit you always drink, and your stomach is built for that greasy shit down at Wong's rat hole!, she said as she laughed out loud. Listen it's not such a bad thing if you are, shit you a married woman and to be honest it might be the best thing for you. Slow your ass down and help you to get your priorities in order. I'm just saying. Go to the drugstore and get you one of those home pregnancy tests and go from there."

"Okay okay, I will if it will make you happy."

"It aint about me, truth be told if you are you need to know now, because if you are you know you have to stop all that extra shit because ummm hello…… we know what kind of damage that can do."

"You right, I kind of thought about it to be honest but just threw the thought back over my shoulders. I would hate for it to be true and I end up fucking up a new life. I'm going downstairs to go take care of that. I'll call you when I get back."

Click.

Mahogany hung up the phone so fast that she didn't even wait for Veronica to respond. She gets dressed pitter-pattered passed Trevor into the living room, looking for her purse; she rolls Jean over practically knocking him off the couch. Jean is startled and catches his grip before he hits the floor.

"Damn! Mahogany fuck I do to you?"

"Oh Jean please cool your fucking heals I'm just trying to find my pocketbook."

"Where are you going?"

"Last time I checked I only had one husband."

She finds her purse and she heads to the front door.

Hold up I might as well leave now, I got things to do. I can't sit around all day with y'all alcoholics." Jean says joking around.

"Man would you please come on! I gotta go, come on Jean move it."

"Well damn, I think I need to recap my question. Where the hell you rushing off to in such a hurry? Do I need to wake my cousin up and have him ask you, since that is the one husband that you do have, like you said?"

"I'm going to see a man about a fucking dog, now let's go!"

Jean finishes tying his shoes and he skips down the hall at Mahogany's command. They both walk out the door. She goes one direction and Jean goes another. She walks into the drugstore pacing the aisles with a nervous jitter looking for the home pregnancy test and she couldn't find it. She goes over to the counter clerk and asks for help.

"Excuse me, can you tell me where I can find the home pregnancy test?"

"Sure, give me one moment."

"I hate to bother you, but I tried looking for it myself and for the life of me, I just couldn't find it."

"It's okay; we keep them behind the counter these days. We've had a few incidents where they mysteriously cleared the shelves along with a few other things."

"Yeah I know what you mean. Can't have anything that holds more value than a cup of water these days."

"Exactly. Okay so we have this, this and this."

"Well which one is more accurate?"

"Here this is one of the most popular ones, EPT."

"How do I use it?"

"Well it's a simple one step process, you pee in a cup, you take the little absorbent tip and dip it and wait for 2 minutes and if there are 2 blue lines showing a plus sign then you're pregnant."

"Okay, that sounds simple enough. I guess it's better than the rabbit era."

"The rabbit era? What's that?"

"Well many many years ago, before your time and mines they would take the urine from a woman and inject it into a female rabbit and if it caused the rabbit to ovulate then that meant that the woman is pregnant. But they stopped doing that because the lives of too many rabbits were being sacrificed."

"Oh wait a minute, there's a song by Aerosmith called sweet emotion and there's a part where he says, "You can't catch me cause the rabbit done died."

"Exactly, you're right."

"I always wondered what the heck he was talking about."

Mahogany laughs. "Well now you know, and now it's time for me to know. Girl wish me luck whatever it may be."

"Good luck."

"Thank you for taking time out to help me have a good day."

"Okay take care, you too."

Mahogany exits the store and heads straight home. As soon as she gets home she goes right to the bathroom and takes the test.

DUET

BY: DEZ SABREE

CHAPTER ONE

"Trevor wake up baby I got good news, Trevor get up! We're having a baby!"

She tried poking, and shaking him but Trevor didn't move an inch. He was always a very hard sleeper especially after a long night of nonstop drinking and drugging. Mahogany is so wound up she boldly stands over Trevor forcefully yanking him off the bed, with her petite 5"2 125lb frame, coco brown skin, curly jet black hair and the biggest smile which seemed to bring in a bright ray of light. She is waving the home pregnancy test in the air. Trevor staggers trying to catch his balance, while struggling to gain focus with one bloodshot eye open.

"What did you say?"

"I said we're having a baby!"

Trevor stands there collecting his thoughts as he reaches out grabbing hold of the test strip with the blue positive sign. The thought of being a father would periodically cross Trevor's mind but he was always so busy getting high that he didn't make it his main concern at the time, but without a doubt he was very happy.

Mahogany suffered the same co-dependency but she always said she wanted to have a kid before she would turn thirty. They stood in the middle of the floor holding on to one another with tender-hooks. Mahogany knew right away it was time to make new life changing decisions.

All night she impatiently paced the floors contemplating her next big step, which was to give up the drinking and drugging. She knew that this time kicking the habit would have to be done with professional assistance. The following day she searched the yellow pages found B.T.C (Brooklyn Treatment Center) located downtown Brooklyn on Jay Street. Mahogany was the type of woman who had a natural beauty and she made it her business, fiend or not to stay looking good. She put on her most flattering outfit, tip toeing pass Trevor making her way down the corridor.

"Yo Mae Mae Where the fuck you going?" Trevor calls out with a raspy tone emerging from his throat followed by a loud dry cough.

"Looking all good and shit."

"I made an appointment with B.T.C."

"Oh Ok, I see you really serious about this shit aint you?"

He says with a chuckle in his voice and slight grin on his mug. She turns to Trevor with an expression like she had just gotten kicked in the teeth.

Fiddling around in her purse mumbling under her breath, "My keys, my wallet, my ID, Ok I'm good."

She reaches the front door. Loudly clearing her throat she utters strongly.

"I've never been more serious about anything in my entire life and its either you with me or you not." and she slams the front door.

Trevor was the type of man who either knew the right things to say or the wrong. When he was high he was a different man, a happier man, when he wasn't high he was on edge a lot, and can be very sarcastic. Chasing after her, he stops her in her tracks.

"Mae Mae I'm sorry, you know I didn't mean it like that." Towering over her he stands about 6"2 Slender but muscular build dark complexion and miniature afro.

"What I mean to say is that I'm proud of you, I'm happy for us, I love you and I am with you every step of the way."

"I'm just a little scared because I know what I have to do. You can't do this on your own baby I'm fiend out and now I have to do to the right thing and walk away from the bullshit. It's gonna take time for me, however I'm gonna do it, but on my own, and I promise. I won't bring any of that shit in front of you. And besides you're carrying Trevor Jr."

"Trevor Jr.?"

Right away she cuts him off.

"No disrespect Trevor but I already thought up a name for our son."

"And what's that?"

"Prezden."

"Prezden? What the fuck is that?"

"He's gonna be the 1st black President of the United States, or at least that's how people would look up to him."

"We can talk about that later now go and handle your business with your sexy ass!"

For the 1st time in a long time Trevor talked with good sense while sober. Mahogany had an undying love for him and she could never imagine life without him.

CHAPTER TWO

She arrives at B.T.C waiting to be called. "Mahogany Dubois!" A short round white woman with dusty blonde hair calls out her name.

"Have a seat, my name is Ms. Greene. Now is it Ms. or Mrs. Dubois?"

"Its Mrs. But please just call me Mahogany."

"M a h o g a n y ", Ms. Greene repeats slowly stretching out every alphabet in her name.

"Isn't that the name of a movie?"

"Yeah." Nodding her head, Mahogany responds with a shy tone to her voice.

"Who played in that movie umm?"

Struggling with her words looking down thru her bifocals and her head slightly tilted.

"Was it Debra, Donna?"

"It's Dianna, Dianna Ross." Mahogany swiftly interrupts ending with a curt sigh. They both give a short smile then get right down to business.

"So Mahogany (quick smile) what brings you here today?"

"Well I recently discovered that I am with child and truth to the matter is I have a heavy addiction to dope and for my baby's survival as well as my own I really need to make a positive change and rid this from my life."

"How long have you been using?"

"Off and on for about 3 years now."

"Have you ever attended a drug treatment program before?"

" No , I've tried several times to fight this demon on my own, 2 months clean here, 4 months in and something always seems to weaken me and draw me right back to it."

"So what's different this time?"

"Well the 1st step, which is the biggest step of all, is that I'm here. As I mentioned before I am pregnant and I want to give my child a clean start in his life."

"Him? You're hardly showing. How do you know what you're having already?"

"I just know in my heart, Ms. Greene I'm just tired of falling prey to this sort of life and the negativity it has brought my way."

"What about your husband?"

"He is willing to support me in any way possible."

"Does he use also?"

"Yes but he has never had the desire to stop until now, so he's never made an effort to try, but now he is willing to try."

"Oh is he here? Will he be enrolling?"

"No! He's decided to do things in his own way he's going cold turkey. He is a strong believer that whatever he puts his mind to doing he can do it."

"What made you start using in the 1st place?"

"I started hanging out with my husband, his clique of friends, and some family members, but most of all following his path."

"Yeah, drinking and drugging are learned behaviors' and a choice. We're here to present an endless solution to abuse problems. Our program is intended for individuals with significant mental health issues or substance abuse troubles who aspire to the change the direction of their lives. We offer outpatient treatment and we are classified the most successful center for these programs in the state of New York."

DUET

"I need you to fill out this application, complete it from front to back, have a seat in area number 2 and someone will call you."

Mahogany sits there in such deep thought imagining what her new life would be like. It was like she was watching a motion picture in her head..

"Mahogany Dubois", her name is called. Slowly rising up from her seat she makes her way to the back, taking a deep breath she mumbles to herself.

"I brought the ticket so now I have to take the ride."

CHAPTER THREE

Mahogany struggled day to day but she continued with her group
therapy, individual therapy and slowly learning how to manage her future. She went to every Dr.'s appt. sometimes with Trevor and sometimes not.

"Trevor we don't talk like we used to. I thought we were working things out. I tried not to get into this right now, but I am just starting to get comfortable with myself and here you are still using. Time is running out, my due date is creeping up and the baby will be here soon, is this the kind of example you want to set for our Son?"

Trevor sits there obviously hung over and emotionless with his head in his hand.

"Mae Mae I know I fucked up but it aint nothing I can't fix. I know that my getting high has interfered with a lot and I'm a little backed up on the taxes but I give you my word we gonna be back on track in no time."

Trevor inherited a beautiful spacious one family home from his Grandfather, in the Clinton hills section of Brooklyn , paid in full all he had to do was keep up with the taxes. This was one of the best things they had going for them and Trevor fell by the waist side because of his addiction.

"I don't want you worrying about this too much because I am going to do whatever I need to do to make this right. The only thing I want you to do is concentrate on is this right here."

He says while rubbing Mahogany's football shaped belly.

Trevor stepped up to the plate doing all kinds of odds and end type jobs, in addition to getting a job at Fred's auto mechanic shop just up the street. He stayed so busy that he didn't find much time to get high.

In view of the fact that Trevor made the most of his time working at Fred's, doing a lot of overtime Fred was so impressed that he gave Trevor a 1963 Chevy conversion van. It was a shabby color blue, it had a few dents and worn tires and a few minor rust spots here and there. It had a lot of wear and tear and needed some work , but Trevor had the ability to bring it back to life. In a short time he had it on the road running and looking good. On the weekends he and Mahogany would go for long quiet rides listening to one of her favorite artist named John Lennon. They were both fans of Lennon; it seems that a lot of his songs had some bearing on their life in some way or another.

Her favorite songs were "Love, Imagine and Stand by Me". Trevor would frequently listen to Woman and most of all cold Turkey. He listened to cold Turkey day and night. It helped give him inspiration with kicking his drug habit.

"Mae Mae pick up the phone it's Veronica!" Trevor yells out. Veronica was Mahogany's close childhood friend and she was expected to be Prezden's God-Mother. Although Veronica resided in New Jersey and lived a totally different lifestyle she and Mahogany talked frequently on the telephone and would get together on birthdays, special occasions and most holidays.

DUET

Veronica was a beautiful curvaceous woman who stood about 5"10, long dark brown hair that flowed down the middle of her back. She had the most beautiful grey eyes you could ever imagine and golden-brown skin tone. When Veronica was a young girl only just a teen she was raped by her Step-Father. The rape was so brutal and damaging that it left her with the scar of not being able to bear children. Since then this has left her incapable of trusting men and having any productive relationship with them. As she grew older she became promiscuous, she would just use guys for whatever she wanted at the time and wouldn't think twice about them later. She received a lot of compliments and promises from the men she would come into contact with. Veronica became the type of woman who loved to have the finer things in life and working a 9-5 or sitting in anyone's educational institution just wasn't the thing for her to do. She began prostituting shortly after graduating high school. Her motto was God gave me the beauty why not use it to my advantage.

Since she wasn't going to have children she believed she could be as fault-finding as she wanted to be since she didn't have anyone to depend on her then and no one to leave behind whenever she depart life . Veronica was a high class call girl; her Evan Picone heels never grazed the sidewalks of the red light district. She had her little black book that she referred to as her information bank, filled with names, telephone numbers and addresses of her gentleman callers which were Doctors, Lawyers, Sports figures, Stock Brokers etc.. She wore the most expensive clothing, dined in the finest restaurants , she lavished herself with exaggerated jewelry, a beautiful 2 bedroom condo in the upper part of Montclair in New Jersey and every time you look up she was traveling somewhere across the world.

"Hello?"

"Hey V how you doing?"

The two carry on a conversation that lasted almost an hour. They talked about anything under the sun. They finally set a date on when Veronica would come down to hang about until Mahogany went into labor.

Since Veronica was to be the Godmother she definitely wanted to be there for the big day. Because Veronica was her own boss and had over generous clients she could afford to take the time off from the trade "as she would call it" and pick up where she left off upon her return. Mahogany's due date was November 30th so they decided on the week before. Unfortunately, Mahogany began to experience complications and spent a few days in the hospital and was put on bed rest. Veronica changed plans and initiated her stay much sooner.

"Trevor there's a taxi outside I think its V, go meet her at the door."

Trevor and his cousin Jean had been up half the night drinking Jack Daniels and he was still feeling a tad intoxicated. The doorbell rang before Trevor could finish tying his shoes. Adding a little pep to his step Trevor struggled to hide his slight stagger so he wouldn't be in hot water with Mahogany. Trevor comes within a few inches of the foyer, piercing the silence the doorbell rings again.

"Hold up V I aint running marathons girl, I'm coming, I'm coming."

Trevor opens the door and there Veronica stood wearing a full length mink coat, diamonds glistening from each earlobe, the scent of her perfume that softly rushed the hallway, her matching Gucci luggage set and a pair of sunglasses that nearly covered her whole face.

"Damn girl whose Island you done been on now? You coming up in here looking all Hollywood and shit!"

"What's up T?"

She greets Trevor with a big hug and kiss drops her bags and heads straight down the corridor, yelling out, "Where's my girl? Oh my God Mae Mae look at you! You look so beautiful."

Rubbing her stomach.

"Girl you are all baby, yeah this is a boy, they say you can tell by the shape of a woman's stomach, it's shaped like a football. You make pregnancy look glamorous girl."

Mahogany was so excited that Veronica was there she kept the biggest smile on her face. They chatted about so much stuff, updated each other on what's been going on in their lives, to the latest gossip of shared acquaintances, and they stayed glued to the TV set watching the latest turn of events of their favorite drama filled night time soap opera called "Dallas." Anxiously waiting to find out who shot Jr. they both shouted from the rooftops when they learned that it was his sister in law, Kristin Shepard, who had done it.

Veronica took good care of Mahogany she waited on her hand and foot, she was a great cook and knew how to clean the hell out of a house. She really didn't want Mahogany to do much of anything except relax and get ready for her big day. Trevor really did appreciate all that Veronica was doing and it eased his mind a lot while he went to work and did what he needed to do financially to make ends meet. Veronica is awakened by the aroma of freshly cooked food. She gradually makes her way to the kitchen. Mahogany had put together quite an assortment of foods. There was crisp bacon, sausage, scrambled eggs, biscuits hot from the oven, tea brewing on the stove top, fresh fruit and a bloody Mary cocktail for Veronica since this is how she started her day out on the regular.

"Mahogany please you shouldn't have, you ought to be resting and you know this."

"I know but I've been feeling impatient all night. I've been getting small contractions here and there but didn't want to call for any false alarms, so I decided to keep myself busy."

"Oh my God girl you know you]re about to have this baby."

Veronica is looking around the place noticing the furniture in the baby's room has been change around.

"Most people say that when a woman is about to go in they do strange stuff like this. How often are you getting the contractions? Are you in pain? Why didn't you wake me? Oh my God, Should I wake Trevor?"

"Damn V calm down it's not that serious, at least not yet anyway.

The contractions are coming but not that strong right now, they just feel like slight menstrual cramps, sit down enjoy breakfast, and I'll wake Trevor, be right back."

After breakfast Trevor takes a quick shower and heads out the door.

A half hour passes and the contractions are coming closer.

"V call down to Fred's and tell Trevor it's time. My water just broke we need to get to the hospital now."

Trevor flew home like a bat out of hell. Driving like he was in a foreign Country, he broke almost every traffic rule there is, they made it to Brookdale hospital in record time. Within 30 minutes of arriving to the hospital a baby boy is born, Prezden Trevor Dubois, December 8, 1980 6 lbs. 11 ounces 19 inches this has now marked the beginning of their new family unit.

CHAPTER FOUR

Both Trevor and Mahogany's family were nearly nonexistent, each did not have siblings. Other than a few distant cousins, unhealthy aunts and uncles he barely knew just about everyone in Trevor's family had passed away. Once it became obvious that Mahogany was getting high, her family tried several times to make her end the relationship with Trevor. Her parents had exhausted to giving her an ultimatum to leave Trevor for good and come home or to continue with him and they would wash their hands of her. Clearly she continued her relationship with Trevor.

As soon as visiting hours began Veronica was right there. She walks in the door with balloons, a giant gift basket with goodies for Mother and Son. She is tickled pink when the nurse brings Prezden into the room. She briskly rushes to the bathroom and washes her hands so she can hold him. Immediately she is head over heels for the new addition to the family.

Trevor went downstairs to the café to grab a cup of coffee and newspaper. Trevor is disturbed by what he saw. Headline news John Lennon is shot to death in front of his apartment building by a crazed fan. Since he is a Lennon fan he is understandably upset. He returns to the room, "This is fucked up! Somebody killed Lennon last night!"

"What are you talking about Trevor?" Mahogany asks with a very confused look on her face. Mahogany is holding Prezden in her arms, so Trevor hands the newspaper to Veronica and she reads the story aloud.

JOHN LENNON SHOT DEAD

Former Beatle John Lennon has been shot dead by an unknown gunman who opened fire outside the musician's New York apartment. The 40-year-old was shot several times as he entered the Dakota, his luxury apartment building on Manhattan's Upper West Side, opposite Central Park, at 2300 local time.

He was rushed in a police car to St Luke's Roosevelt Hospital Center, where he died. His wife, Yoko Ono, who is understood to have witnessed the attack, was with him. Shots heard a police spokesman said a suspect was in custody, but he had no other details of the shooting. "This was no robbery," the spokesman said, adding that Mr. Lennon was probably shot by a "deranged" person.

Witness reports say at least three shots were fired and others have claimed they heard six. There are also reports Mr. Lennon staggered up six steps into the vestibule after he was shot, before collapsing. Jack Douglas, Lennon's producer, said he and the Lennon's had been at a studio called the Record Plant in Mid-town earlier in the evening and Lennon left at 2230. Mr. Lennon said he planned to have some dinner and then return home, Mr. Douglas said.

Over the next few days spent in the hospital this seemed to be the talk all around. Mahogany and Trevor were crushed by the news because the two were big Lennon fans. Lennon's Murder was followed by an outstanding amount of grief across the world on an unimaginative scale. At least three Beatle fans committed suicide after the murder. Lennon's wife (Ono) made a public appeal asking mourner's not to give into despair. Ono sent word to the fans that a silent ten minute prayer vigil will be held in Central Park the following Sunday .

"Congratulations!"

Shouts chimed out as Mahogany and Trevor entered their home. Veronica and Trevor had put together a surprise coming home party for Mahogany. The room was filled with neighbors, friends, a few of Trevor's relatives and Co-workers, including Ms. Greene from B.T.C. Mahogany was especially surprised to see Ms. Greene.

"Congratulations across-the-board Mahogany, I bet it took the wind out of your sails." she says with a quiet laughter followed by a loud snort.

"Oh you sure did Ms. Greene; it's so good to see you."

Mahogany is so surprised and happy to see everyone. She gives each person the opportunity to hold baby Prezden, they open gifts, listen to soft music and ate some of the best food, catered by the finest soul food restaurant in town called "Aunt Neva's."

On Dec. 14th 1980 Millions of people around the world responded to Ono's request to pause for 10 minutes of silence to remember Lennon. Thirty thousand gathered in Liverpool, and over 225,000 gathered in Central Park close to the scene of the shooting. During those ten minutes every radio station in NYC went off the air Veronica, Trevor, Mae Mae and Jean stood in the living room holding hands participating in their own silent moment of prayer. It was time for Veronica to return home. Mahogany was saddened by this because she knew she was really going to miss her terribly.

CHAPTER FIVE

They kept in touch more often than ever and Veronica constantly flooded the post office with gifts for Prez. Mahogany made frequent trips to New Jersey to visit Veronica, especially once she and Trevor started having problems again.

"How come every time we have a little problem now, all you wanna do is run to New Jersey and stay with V?"

"How come you keep letting Con Edison turn of the gas and electric?"

"How come there's barely any food in the fridge? How come you still getting high?"

"How come I haven't slapped the shit out of your little ass yet? You must be crazy talking to me like that Mae Mae."

"Fuck you Trevor!"

"I'm telling you Woman it's headed your way."

Trevor is holding his hand in the air with the back end facing Mahogany.

"Oh so now I'm supposed to be scared Trevor? Scared like you? You scared to hear the truth you just a sorry ass."

(Slap) out of the blue Mahogany collapsed to the floor. Kicking and screaming. She is instantly flooded with tears.

"Are you happy now? Does this make you feel like a fucking man now? You just hit your fucking wife."

Running into the kitchen grabbing the biggest and heaviest cast iron pan she charges after Trevor as he runs down the hallway to exit the house. Slam!! (He makes it out the front door in a nick of time.)

"Okay! Now go nose fuck with your friends, I fucking hate you for this Trevor!"

Mahogany called Veronica and immediately let her in on what just happened. She packed her and Prezden a bag and went straight to New Jersey, this time she stayed nearly three weeks.

Boom!

"What the fuck was that?"

V and Mae Mae shout out as they dash down the hallway toward the front window to see what the loud crashing sound was. "Damn it Trevor what the hell are you doing here?"

Trevor is standing in front of V's house in the pouring rain, with the van still running, crashed in one side, and with the front light completely busted out.

"You see this is the type of shit!'

"Mae Mae!" Trevor roars out cutting her off, holding his face with a ridiculous looking squint, face frowned hard, mouth curled tight, with a wet cigarette hanging limp from the right corner of his lips.

"Bring yo ass down here now woman! We need to talk."

"Trevor don't do this in front of the house, you're right you and Mae Mae do need to talk, but not through my living room window, this aint no fucking Romeo and Juliet. Park the car and I will buzz you in."

Trevor staggers his way up the spiral staircase barely making his way to the top. Veronica opens the door, looking Trevor up and down with a disappointed look on her face.

"Listen Trevor, Mae Mae is in the back making sure Prezden is okay, but before she comes out just remember respect my house and only cats have 9 lives."

"What the fuck is that supposed to mean V? What you and my wife been in here doing for 3 weeks? You start to look more like a Designer Dyke talking that shit to me."

Mae Mae over hears the commotion, so she quickly makes her way down the hallway before things get deeper. As she and Veronica were passing one another down the hallway, Veronica whispers in her ear, "Girl it's not the man in your life, it's the life in your man."

"Mae Mae I'm up shits creek without a paddle, I miss you and Prezden, and y'all have to come home baby."

"Trevor I can't keep doing the same old thing over and over, Trevor you full of piss and vinegar. I take two steps forward and you take two steps back."

"Mae Mae set your mind at rest, I had a lot of time to think and figure this shit out, you and Prezden come first, you and Prezden come first you and Prezden come first."

"What the fuck you keep repeating yourself for?"

"So you will know I'm serious. What I tell you 3 times is true."

"Listen Trevor you are my husband and of course I want to make this work, but you have to be serious about what you are saying. I mean come on I have been clean since the day I learned I was pregnant with Prezden and he is turning a year soon. It's time you get it together to."

"I'm here and I'm determined, so come on get your stuff and let's go home .But wait I owe V a big apology, that's my girl to and I need to apologize to her straight from the shoulder."

Walking back and forth with a nervous jitter, Trevor calls out to Veronica.

"Hey V, I just want to say I'm sorry for, slight hesitation in his voice, ummm well."

"Look Trevor I didn't lose my face behind it and it will take more than a one- liner to do that, I accept your apology."

Veronica steps down the hallway with Prezden in her arms handing him over to Trevor. Prezden lays there in his Father's arms half- awake with the cutest little smile you ever did see.

"Should I call a taxi?" with laughter in V's voice "Because from the looks of things I don't think that bat mobile will make it back to Brooklyn."

"That was well deserved V", Trevor smiles "but nah we'll be fine."

They get in the van and drive off, Mae Mae looks in the back seat and Trevor has a bunch of boxes piled up in the back.

"Trevor what's all that stuff back there?"

"Oh that's some stuff me and Jean brought from the Jews down on Delancey. You know these past few weeks that you been gone me and Jean been trying to make moves. I have something back there that I'm sure you will enjoy."

With a big smile that lit up her whole face.

"Oh yeah what's that?"

"It's a VCR."

"You mean one of them things that I can watch movies at home?"

"Yes baby."

"Oh my God! Thank you baby!"

"Ooh I can't wait to get home now. What made you get one of those? Was it expensive? How the heck did you afford this?"

"Listen don't worry we got a deal on a lot of goods on Delancey and don't worry no cops are gonna come knocking on the door. Jean had got one a ways back and while you were gone I was going over to Auntie Mildred and Jeans watching movies and shit, you know anything to keep me busy as I can. I can't tell you how many times we watched Scarface. I know that movie word for word line for line see what you done did?"

Turning his head looking at her with a raised eyebrow.

"I heard they are going to remake that movie real soon.

Different actors and everything of course. Well I hope it's as good as the original I tell you that Paul Muni plays the hell out of his role as Tony Camonte. That's my dude."

"I know Aunt Mildred must have been having a fit with y'all watching that gangster smut up in her house."

"Nah she was kool. She aint bothered with us."

"So when we get home can we watch some smut of our own?" Rubbing his hand across Mae Mae's thigh giving her the eye.

"See Trevor sitting here messing with you I'm gonna have to put my birth control glasses on lol."

"What?"

"Yes keep looking at me like that and I'll end up pregnant."

"So you wanna practice on the birth control hole?"

Laughing out loud

"What the hell is that?"

"You know the other whole, hint hint."

"Eew Trevor you nasty it's either my birth crack or nothing at all."

Covering Prezden's ears

"Alright enough of the blue humor we have little ears in our presence."

"Okay okay, give me a kiss can I at least get that?"

"Here Trevor yes you may."

Leaning in planting a soft quick kiss on his lips, "Oh Trev what you got toothpaste hangover or something?" wiping her lips.

"Laughing out loud.... Ha-ha you funny!"

"Not funny enough cause soon as we get home I'm throwing some brain bleach on you so you can forget that last freaky thought of yours." She said laughing out loud.

"You gonna do it." Poking her in her side.

"Stop Trevor"

She busts out laughing

They continue to laugh and joke the entire ride home.

"I can tell you wanna do it, you gonna do it."

Trevor laughs out loud turning up the radio to one of their favorite songs "The long winding road", by the Beatles

CHAPTER SIX

Over the next couple of months things were continuously on the up and on the down. Mahogany began to lose hope and patience with Trevor. He end up getting fired from Fred's after an altercation with a customer and Trevor was obviously drunk and high at the time. He wasn't keeping up with the bills and they were in a lot of jeopardy. Mahogany had to make the decision to find gainful employment because depending on Trevor just wasn't cutting the mustard.

She got a job working down at a local supermarket doing cashier work. Trevor had a lot of objections but that didn't stand strong simply because he wasn't living up to his responsibilities. During the morning hours while Mae Mae worked at Cinco Supermercados Estrella's, Prezden stayed home with Trevor. Jean would come over and hang out with Trevor and as they would sip and scheme up big money plans.

"Yo Trevor I'm about to get up on some shit next month and I wanna put you down."

"What kind of shit you talking about Jean?"

"Well I know this dude down in Philly and he moving some shit back and forth from state to state and he need a few runners.

There's big money in it for me and I know you going through your shit right now and you aint really feeling Mae Mae being down at that bullshit ass supermarket what the fuck is the name again?" laughing out loud licking his lips preparing for pronunciation "Cinco Supermercados Estrella's hahahahaha!"

"Eh Yo Jean do that shit again", Trevor says as he laughs into a nasty dry hacking cough.

"Ok ok", squinting his eyes licking his lips while shaking one leg to the side "Cinco Supermercados Estrella's!" They both begin to laugh hysterically…

"Ok, let's get back on point, we aint right. Anyway so I figured hey you my cousin let me put you on right quick so you can do you and get back on the right track."

"Ok, but Jean what type of shit" dry raspy cough, "you talking about?"

"He's moving coke and weed."

"Okay go on hit me in the head, chat the fuck up Cuzzo!"

The two get to talking so intensely that neither one of them paid attention when Mae Mae walked in the door.

"Baby I'm home!" her voice springs echoing the walls down the long corridor.

"Trev ……. Come help me with these bags, Trevor? What the hell."

Setting the bags down on the floor she makes her way down the hallway. Trevor and Jean sitting there talking up a quiet storm.

"Damn Trevor you aint hear me calling you?"

"Sorry baby me and Jean sitting here brainstorming on some brilliant shit right here."

"Oh yeah well Ein and Stein I have a brilliant ideal. Howz about y'all grab them bags so I can put this food away and start getting things ready for Prez's Birthday Party this evening?" laughing as Trevor smacks her directly on the ass.

"What you do that for?"

"Cause them steps you were taking were looking illegal girl had to stop you in them tracks, lucky Jean here otherwise I would arrest that ass hahaha!" Walking away cracking that little half smile that always seems to drive Trevor crazy for her, she answers the phone and it's V.

"Hey V, girl I hope you calling to say you're on your way over here."

"I'm waiting for black car I should be there in the next two hours or so."

"Listen, do you have everything you need? Because once I get on my travels I don't want to have to make any extra stops."

"Bring a bottle of that fancy red wine you had the last time and I'm good thanks. "

"Ooh girl you mean one of our favorite solutions to life's problems? I got it right here in my bag." They chatter a few moments later then Mahogany tends to Prez.

The party turned out well, some neighbors and their children attended, Ms. Greene, V, Jean, a few of Trevor's aunts and cousins and they partied till the late night hours. Veronica brought Prez an avalanche of gifts; it looked like she should be filing for bankruptcy the very next day. She spared no expenses when it came to Prez.

"Trevor I noticed you and Jean spent a lot of time yesterday back and forth on the phone, who were y'all talking to?"

"Oh remember me and Jean working on something that's gonna put dough back in this house, get us back on track and you don't have to leave out and go to that damn supermarket, wait a minute how Jean say that shit again?"

"Cinco Supermercados Estrella's hahaha "

"You know what Trevor you really make yourself look extra childish. You and fucking Jean making fun of where I work to make ends meet cause your black ass running around here trying to buy a fucking pony."

"A Pony? What the fuck are you talking about Mae Mae?"

"I mean you trying to reach the impossible at the rate Yo ass going you gonna end up in jail. Watch a little Scarface and now you and Jean taking shit and running with it. I mean can't you find something else to do like hunt Alligators or something." She mumbles under her breath.

"At least I can get a handbag and shoes out the deal."

"Ok, seriously Mae Mae I don't really like you in that place anyway, you basically the only black ass mother fucker in there Well non Spanish speaking mother fucker up in there and I don't like that. They probably be talking shit in front cha face all day long and you will never know a damn thing."

Shaking her head ignoring the last comment he just made turning to him with a low pitch in her voice, "Well Trevor I hope this aint nothing illegal because I'm trying to stay on a clear path in life these days and we don't need the bull crap. So what is it that y'all are working on?"

"Mae Mae you tell me what in life aint illegal!"

"What? Listen Trevor……"

"No Mae Mae you listen, I aint got time for this right now, worried about what's legal and illegal. Hell…. there's illegal fireworks, people still get their hands on them, let's see, illegal lane change, people make any chance they get, oh illegal fire arms, almost every house in Brooklyn have one, oh illegal abortion well that's a whole another story, oh and not to forget about those illegal mommy's and poppy's barely speaking English you call coworkers, running around in that lil supermarket you call a job these days. Wait; wait how Jean say that shit again?"

About to get into character she cuts him off, “Fuck you Trevor don’t start with the unnecessary!”

“Ok well Cinco Supermercados Estrella’s you work at every damn day. I’m hungry, and I’m gonna eat that money sandwich no matter what you talking about.”

Trevor storms out the house slamming the door so hard that it knocked two of their wedding pictures straight off the wall. Sharp sounds of glass shattering the floors sent a sudden disturbance in the air that Mae Mae had grew to become very familiar with. Sending her over the edge screaming out.

“I can’t take this shit no more!!” Crying out so loud that it woke Prezden up from his afternoon nap flooded by instant tears. She knew decisions had to be made especially now that she has this delicate young child to tend to. Mahogany started to feel the pressures more than ever and it started taking a toll on her mental health.

CHAPTER SEVEN

She didn't want to keep turning to V, because she just didn't want burden her with the same old issues. She began fighting her demons alone trying not to relapse and get high. She started holding a lot inside. She learned how to cope with her problems and still face the world with a smile on her face. She and Trevor started to grow apart and they saw less and less of each other. Either he was running the streets with Jean coming home late at night or when he was home he basically stayed in a drunk or drug induced coma.

It's 7am the next morning and Trevor has not made it home. Mae Mae is really upset and worried at the same time. He has done many things wrong but to not come home and not call was new on the list. Mae Mae had to be at work in the next 2 hrs. She tried calling Jeans house and got no answer. Her emotions were running high from anger to fear and back again. She called two of Trevor's Aunts and neither one has heard a word from him.

"When he bring his black ass in this house I'm gonna fucking kill him!"

Two hours go by and not a word from Trevor. Mae Mae calls her job and informs them that she has a family emergency and will not be coming in. Within moments of hanging up the phone the phone rings. Dashing down the hallway with Prez on her left hip she makes it to the phone.

"Hello?" Slight pause. Computer voice recording:

This is Riker's Island Correctional Facility with a collect call from….. Inmate, Trevor Dubois press 1 to accept or 2 to decline. Her hands immediately began to shake uncontrollably. With a hysterical tone in her voice she screams out "Trevor what the fuck?"

"I know Mae Mae but listen I'm okay. I fucked up I know me and Jean both up in this bitch! Some shit went down listen I don't want to talk about it on the phone, I need you to come up here so we can talk face to face."

"I can't believe this fucking shit!!! I said this was gonna happen. Damn it Trev and where the hell are you? What fucking Island?"

Mumbling under his breath "Damn sure aint Gilligan's anyway get a pen write all this shit down. The address is 15-00 Hazen Street, East Elmhurst NY."

"Ok.", as she begins writing.

"Take the B38 to Tillary Street, walk down to Fulton and Jay take the F train towards Jamaica 179th street Queens Bridge."

"What the fuck Trevor! "

"Listen I aint got a lot of time on this damn line so listen. Then walk to 21st and 41st Avenue and take the Q100 towards Riker's Island then once you get here you will know. So listen my visiting day is Tuesday. Make sure you have your ID and don't bring a whole lot of shit with you cause they real fucked up in here and they will turn you back around. Oh yeah and Mae Mae call Aunt Mildred, Jean's Mother, might as well let her know what's going on with Jean to while you're at it."

She calls Trevor's Aunt Mildred and lets her know about what it happening. Mildred begged her to keep Prezden while she goes because she didn't feel comfortable with him going to a place like that. Mildred was one of the few relatives left in the family tree and she was sickly. She had emphysema and stayed with an oxygen mask plastered to her face. It was a sad sight to see because this woman had a lot of zest in life but was limited because of her illness. Emphysema ran in the family, a lot of her own brother's and sister's actually died from this disease.

Mahogany agreed to let Prezden stay with her and on Tuesday Morning she brought him over to Mildred's house. She tightly clung to the piece of paper in her hand with the directions she had written down. By the time she got on the Q100 she met a woman named Lisa who was traveling to see her boyfriend. Lisa was a seasoned Veteran at this point. Her man Chaz has been in Ryker's for the past nine months.

The two get to talking, "So what's your man in for?"

"Chaz is a hot head, he was speeding and a cop tried to pull him over in an unmarked car so Chaz kept going. The cop cornered him in and he didn't know it was a cop so he immediately jumped out the car and started going blow for blow with the cop and he end up knocking him out, sending him straight into a coma."

"Oh my God! Are you serious?"

"Yes girl serious as the stank on this bus."

"No disrespect but your man sound crazier than that husband of mine."

"Girl none taken. Anyway you looked a little nervous about being here so let me give you some knowledge on what's yet to come. Before we even get to the main building, you have to lock up any personals that you have. Lipstick, lotion, keys, cigarettes, lighters, hair pins, any little trinkets, rubber bands, and hair thingies anyway you get the point. The lockers are 50 cents so I hope you have change. Then they give you a little bucket to put all your stuff in like your shoes, belt, wallet bag and stuff like that and have to go thru the 1st set of metal detectors. You have to get an identification card to visit the house where your husband is housed. After that you get on another bus that will take you directly there. Then there are 2 more metal detectors to go thru and you will have to take off all that stuff again. Then you wait at anywhere from ten minutes to hours to be called for the visit. The process can take at least three hours and the visit is only one hour and it goes by really fast. So whatever you need to say remember time is not on your side."

They arrived on the Island and things went exactly the way that Lisa had described. Mahogany is called for the visit. Trevor sits there with his hands clasped together and little beads of sweat bursting from his forehead. He was very nervous and he had every right to be. Mahogany spots him and she is walking toward him with smoke blurring vision ready to open fire on him and anyone willing get in the way. She sits down with a stone call stare waiting to hear what Trevor had to say.

"Hey baby" With a short smile drops his head in his hands, "Listen I know you said something like this was gonna happen but listen I" with a long hesitation. "I'm sorry and I just need to get up out of here." Clearing his throat from what almost sound like he wanted to cry. He sits up tall in his seat.

"So is that all that you have to say Trev?"

She says while lightly raising her voice. "Listen I aint about to be sitting up in these monkey bars acting like some little weak as mother fucker, I'm a man from the birth to the death. I know you ready to serve me a storm in a tea cup and listen I understand but first let me tell you what happened from beginning to end then we can chatter fuck till the visit is over."

He leans in close to Mahogany and in a low tone starts to tell her about what happened.

"So the dude in Philly that Jean was getting the connections with, end up switching the operation up at the last minute and had us meet up with these cats up in Queens to pick up some of that stuff. Come to find out him and his ex-girl had a bad break and she set him up with her new dude's connects which was those niggas we met up with. Anyway they end up trying to rob us and next thing I know shit got real crazy. Me and Jean up in some garage fighting these mother fucker's and you know me and I don't back down. I was literally throwing mother fuckers over my back. Then shit got real and I pulled out my joint cause one of them mother fucker's was about to smoke Jean. I hit him once BOP! And he fell. Niggas started scrambling me and Jean managed to get the fuck up out of there. So we running and shit and next thing I know there's cop cars everywhere, bright fucking lights damn near blinding me and these pigs all on top of us with their guns drawn and damn it was over! That whole shit went bad because of some scorned ass bitch!"

"Well Trev you know what they say. Hell hath no fiery than a Woman scorned. Besides Yo ass shouldn't have been there anyway. It's done now so moving forward what they talking? How long you gonna be in this God forsaken place?"

"Well listen I need you to go down to 55 Delancy."

"Delancy? Trevor what's there?"

"Listen Mac Mae I'm explaining it now. So go to 55 Delancey, it's an apartment building. Ring the bell that says Alex Shapiro. That's one of my close Jewish friends. He always told me if I ever needed his help he has a cousin that's a lawyer and he would back me and Jean up. He good on his word so don't worry its kool. Let him know exactly what happened and where I'm at and we good to go."

They continued to talk a few more minutes, leaning in for a hug with a fragile look on her face Mahogany stretches her arms out.

DUET

"Back up!" a strong stern voice is heard a short distance away. It's one of the correction officers assigned to that section of the room. Tapping his watch, with a loud tone in his voice he says wrap it up!

"Ignore him baby we still have time. Didn't they tell you the visit is only an hour?"

"Didn't they ever tell you there's 60 minutes in an hour and we at 55! So back the fuck up and keep your eyes over there." Trevor yells out.

"Keep talking shit and your little lady will be wishing you well."

"Oh yeah? Well did they ever tell a knife without an edge won't work?"

"So what you saying jail bird?"

"I live free or die hard mother fucker that's what I'm saying."

"You must of forgot who I am. You see this uniform, this badge, what it say C.O. Do you know what that stands for?"

"Yeah Cunt overdose!"

"Trevor stop! Kill it already! Damn ignore him, you just allowed him to take three minutes away that we can't get back."

"Yeah listen to her Trevor!"

"Okay Barney Miller."

CHAPTER EIGHT

Trevor and Jean were housed in the same place but it seems they only really got to see one another during meal time and time out in the yard.

"Yo Jean we gotta get the fuck up out of here. I'm telling you shit getting real nasty in here. You know that same C.O I told you about from the other day?"

"Yeah, Daniels right?"

"Yeah. So last night I'm laying in that fucking bacteria bed they call a bunk, and next thing I know he come up in there and take Bunkie out right, so they gone for about an hour. He brings him back and dude was all messed up yo. His face was all bloody and shit, he was limping and he stayed balled over in the corner the rest of the night."

"So Daniels comes back first thing this morning with the other C.O. Martins and they talkin and shit. So Martin asked Bunkie what happened to him, Daniels was like damn looks like you got into some shit with somebody last night huh? You gotta be more careful newbie, you'll be alright you know what I mean? So dude nodding his head up and down. So Martins was like come on I'm gonna take you to the infirmary get you all cleaned up. So he and Martins leave out. So now it's me and Daniels. So Daniels gonna say, if he wasn't a child molester he would probably be an alright guy you know what I mean Trevor?"

" It's funny how some call me and Martins good cop bad cop, but you know in some situations you can either be put on a bad block or the back room. So he shaking his head looking all crazy and shit, looking back at me and he gonna say. " It's all in the balance of my power. So tell me did you see or hear anything last night? You know, anything questionable or worth mentioning to anybody?"

"I looked this mother fucker straight in the eyes and I told him I got my own shit to worry about. My loyalty is to myself and besides people only like dead saints and I refuse to be a Saint or Martyr and you don't seem like you wanna be either one to right?"

"Then he gonna say I like that Trevor you kool. I think we gonna get along pretty well."

"So I don't know what he was getting at so I told him, I aint no boot licker or rat either."

"So what he say after that Cuz?"

"He was like; yeah I don't quite see you as that type but how about a back scratcher?"

"I was about to knock that nigger the fuck out cause I aint know what type of shit he was talking. So I stepped up and was like, what? What you mean with that? He knew what time it was so he slammed the cell door so fast and hard my ears were ringing from that fucked up clanking sound. And when he was on the other side he gonna turn back and say we can talk about that later."

"Trevor listen we gotta get up out of here because aint no happy endings in this shit. What's up with that Lawyer dude from D Street?"

"Well since he was here the other day he told me he was working on some shit, and he supposed to come check you this week. We gotta get up that bail money though and I was spending my doe as fast as I put it in my hands. That's why the night we got caught up in all of this I was really depending on that money for real."

"Yeah and I mean I have a few dollars tucked away at home but you know my Mom's she gonna need to keep her hands on that to take care of things around there."

"Yeah that disability aint enough for Aunt Mildred to survive off for now."

"Damn Trevor we done fucked up this time."

"Well we have to make the best of shit while we here though."

"Mae Mae coming up tomorrow and she bringing Prezden with her, I'm gonna have her put some money on your commissary when she put some in my joint."

Trevor pauses and pulls out a tissue from inside his back pocket
coughing and up chucking just a little phlegm as he says.

"You know we family, we gotta look out for one another."

"Thanks Trev, I appreciate that hey Cuz what's up with that nasty cough? You need to let up on them Marlboros for a while cause that aint sounding good at all.

"Man it's nothing I think I'm coming down with a little cold or something, nothing major but I guess I can ease up on the smokes till this shit passes."

"Yeah good idea because I been noticing that for a while you need to look into that. So check this shit out. After the first call to Tammy and Kim I've been tryna reach both of them and neither one of them accepting any more of my calls. I aint even doing real time and bitches is acting like they too good already. But when I was spending my dollars on them everything was fucking great."

"Yeah well Jean yo ass should of stayed with Niecie anyway she a good woman but you worried about chasing look good, I told you after 2 weeks what I thought of both of them. Tammy was a walking booty and Kim was a talking head especially now, you see that shit don't mean a damn thing."

"When I get out I should crack both of them in their motherfucking heads."

"Whoa Jean you talking dummy right now, end up back in here and this time over some bitches come on you smarter than that. At least right now you can say you up in here cause you was tryna get yours for you and the family."

"Yeah you right Cuz I was just joking anyway and by the way keep that in mind next time you might wanna give Mae Mae the back of them five fingers of death ."

Trevor reaches back in his pocket and pulls out another cigarette. "Alright Jean that was just food from the wise, learn from my mistakes and guess what? Mae Mae would never call the pigs on me."

"Trev come on Cuz man didn't we just talked about them cigarettes?"

"Yeah I know and we just talked about a lot of other shit Jean."

He lights the cigarette and takes a couple of pulls before putting it out.

Mealtime is over and it's time to return to their cells. Daniels is escorting the group back and he starts conversation with Trevor. "What's up Trevor?" Revealing a cigarette he was holding at the tip of his fingers.

"Fuck is that?"

"It's a Marlboro isn't that what you smoke?"

"Well yeah, so what's that all about?"

"Here take it lets walk and talk."

Trevor takes the cigarette and places it down in his sock, relighting the one he previously started smoking. He and Daniels hold a private conversation.

"Listen trust, love and Loyalty. I know doesn't lie behind these walls but you seem like a dependable type of dude and you are about your money and trying to get somewhere in life. You mind your business in here and you don't really fuck with these cats up in here like that except your cousin I did a little of my own research."

Swiftly cutting him off Trevor interrupts.

"Research? What type of shit is that?"

"Hold on Trevor, I don't quite mean it like that. In conversation I found that we both have a friend in common in the free world. He tells me good things about you and I like what I hear so I wanna present some good opportunities for you while you here. You know help you get out here quicker, get your bail money up and something to line my pockets too."

"What is this some kind of joke or something? And what common friend me and you got? And how did I come part of the conversation?"

"Well that weekend after you and I exchanged a few unpleasant words." Daniels explains with a slight grin on his face shaking his head.

"I was at a party and conversation about work came up, something that happens quite often and I shared our little comical exchange of words and as the conversation went further and more questions was asked I come to realize that you know some of the same people I know."

"Ok so who is it? What is it top secret information or something?" Trevor asked with a sarcastic expression planted on his face.

"You know Marco? He lives on Myrtle Ave? They call him Polo? About my height, kinda big, brown skinned got a big mole on his left cheek? Got a sister name." Before he could finish Trevor interrupts.

"Kayla? Hell yeah I know him, that's my nigga!"

Daniel continues and tells Trevor that Marco is married to one of his cousins.

"Who your cousin? You talking about Sabrina?"

"Yeah of course."

Trevor starts laughing interrupted by a nasty coughing spell.

"Hot damn aint that some shit."

"So what type of business are you talking about?"

"First I'm gonna get you and your Cousin on kitchen duty."

"That aint no money, let's see, what's that $10-$25.00 a week?"

"Well that's only where it starts but trust me when I say that the true value of money is how much of it is circulated. Once we get the ball rolling you gonna forget you in jail and it will seem more like you're living in a gated community. "

"Whoa hold up, I been charged not convicted I don't plan on being in here long, but ok sounds good for the in between time I'm with you so far, but shit you aint no different than me."

"What you mean by that?"

"I see you don't have much respect for the law."

"Respect for the law? Ohhhh Trevor see that's the thing, I am the law. You know Rothschild once said, give me control over the nation's money supply and I care not who makes the law."

"Who's that?"

"He was this German banker who founded the Rothschild family International banking dynasty."

"You seem real confident in whatever the plan."

"Shit I like it old money, long money can teach some things on new money gotta start somewhere."

"Exactly."

"Gotta read up on history and learn some things, a lot of cats in here busy burying their faces in Jack books. Spend some time in the library Trevor soaks up some knowledge. Anyway here's the deal, I'm going on vacation for three weeks and when I get back, I will get the details to you. But From this point on we need to continue on as usual. You don't want to be perceived as being friendly with me because in here they will take it as you being a snitch and that can get you killed."

Daniels and Trevor were on their way to a new relationship, and the way things initially started out with them quickly dwindled away. They now have familiar connections and a new understanding on things.

Over the next few days they kept any verbal communication to a minimum. Mae Mae and Prezden continued to visit Trevor on a weekly basis, she even brought Jeans Mother Aunt Mildred on one occasion, it was actually too much for her to handle. Lisa and Mae Mae became travel buddies and their children kept company the whole ride, leaving time for Mae Mae and Lisa to their girl talk.

"Hey babe what ever happened to that Jerk C.O. you know the one with the bad attitude? I haven't seen him standing watch the last couple of few weeks what happened he got fired or something?"

"Nah he's on vacation."

"Well thank God for that."

Trevor leans in her ear and explained the connection he and Daniels have and that he turns out to be an okay dude after all. At first Mae Mae was a little surprised, but it actually set her mind at ease, because this was one less thing she had to worry about. Although, Trevor explained their connection he never bothered to let her in on any of the business arrangements the two were working up.

"So what's happening with the case? "

"They offered me a plea bargain but you know what I don't really want to talk about that shit and get you all upset right now things are going good this is my mess and I tend to get it right."

"I know Trevor I'm trying to get passed that because it's already done but do I need to call John Shapiro and talk to him myself? Put some fire under his heels, tell him get my man up out of here? You have to hurry and come home. This is just too much for me to handle Trevor."

"I know hang in there tho baby, Shapiro is working on getting me and Jean out of here soon. If it wasn't for the lack of money we would both be out on bail. But pretty soon that will all be taken care of and we can worry about the charges thereafter."

"Shapiro actually tried to get me and Jean to act like we didn't understand the charges against us, so that we would have to get placed in a mental institution and take this thing they call a 730 exam."

"What's the purpose of that Trevor?"

"Well if we both aren't competent to stand trial then how can we be punished for something we don't understand? He said if we do that, then there is a chance the charges may be lessened and in some cases dismissed. There's a lot that comes along with something like this tho."

"Such as?"

"Well I aint with acting like I'm crazy and being put in some nut house, and being labeled possibly for the rest of my life. Basically and however I may end up having a hard time re-joining the human race. People hate you when you smart and despise you when you're a fool."

"What do you mean by that Trevor? I thought hate and despise was the same thing?"

"Mae Mae let me tell you like this despise is much stronger than hate. You can hate someone who is superior to you, and dislike them deeply, but despise someone you consider worthless and look down on them."

"That makes sense in a strange kinda way."

"Tell that lawyer of yours to get it right cause aint nobody making my man certifiable. It's bad enough that I feel like I'm losing you every time I leave this place. It's getting harder and harder putting this boy to bed at night, he cries for you. He misses you singing y'all little bedtime song at night, Beautiful Boy. The first couple of nights I tried singing it to him he got so agitated with me he nearly had a fit and went into a crying tantrum right away kicking so hard his lil shoe went flying across the room landed on the night table leaving a crack in the glass. I tell you that little boy has fire in him just like his Daddy and we both know that aint entirely good."

"Pretty soon I will be out of here and free as a bird. Don't worry Mae Mae this will all be over soon."

The visit is almost over and Trevor spends the remaining time to playing and talking to Prezden. Most of the time Prezden is so tired from the long travel that he falls asleep by the time the visit actually begins.

The following morning Daniels returns to work. He goes to Trevor's cell and wakes him up. Dubois let's go, you're moving to the ghetto penthouse referring to the cells located at the top tier. He gives Trevor a certain look and mumbles under his breath that Jean should be expecting a visit from Polo over the next couple of days. Trevor immediately went along with things and didn't bother to question anything. Once Trevor moved to his new cell, he realizes that Jean was moved also and to the cell right next to his. They quickly started communicating thru the vents in the cell.

On Jeans next visiting day he received a visit from Polo.

"Let's make this short and sweet. You and Trev are on kitchen duty I'm sure Daniels explained. There's big money to be made in here and we gotta do this right. I would prefer to talk to Trev cause we go back a long way, but that don't take nothing from you you're his right hand man and I know you good for yours to. So listen y'all gonna be pushing weed up in here but not the traditional way, that's why y'all in the kitchen and making that jailhouse wine to. They say good wine warms people faces but good money warms my heart."

"I'm gonna need you to remember everything I'm about to tell you because we can't take chances right now writing shit down. For the weed we refer to as firecrackers all you need is peanut butter, and those lil fucked up salty damn near stale crackers they give y'all up in here. You spread the peanut butter with a penny size amount of weed on top wrap it in foil place it in one of them extra heavy wool blankets. For the wine that we refer to as Pruno you mix about 10 cups of sugar, 14 cups of orange juice, 2 cups of water and 7 yeast pellets. Use the 5 gallon plastic trash bags as the container and pour everything in there, try to throw in some oranges, grapefruits and shit like that to speed up the process. Put the bag under a blanket tuck that and the firecrackers in whatever dark corner that Daniels tells you to stash and let it sit for a couple of days and you ready for the next step which is to distribute to the buyers on the list that Daniels will provide to you and stick strictly to the list unless Daniels lets you know otherwise."

CHAPTER NINE

The following week, they both started their new jobs. Trevor and Jean began their kitchen duties. Things went smoother than intended. Meanwhile Mae Mae was still trying to keep things together back at home. The loneliness and worry slowly started to take over her thoughts. She would take Prezden over to Mildred's house during the day while she worked. Several times during the week she would pick him up later and later. At first Mildred didn't bother to question things because she figured that with all Mae Mae had been going thru, she probably needed a little time to herself. This one particular evening Mildred noticed a change in Mae Mae's behavior and she decided to say something to her about it.

"Mae Mae, what's going on with you? I mean I know you going thru a lot right now, but I sure hope its only stress got you looking a little worn down lately."

"Worn down? Oh Aunt Mildred please, you can't expect me to look beautiful 24/7. You a woman like me you know how it is." Mae Mae had an unusual nervousness to her and funny look in her eyes.

"Yeah of course I know what it is to deal with the worries of the world basically every day, but I don't know what it is to depend on something that can destroy you in the end."

"And Aunt Mildred exactly what would that be?"

"I'm gonna ask you this once, did you start back getting high again?"

"What kind of question is that?"

"Well it's one that needs an answer and an honest one at that."

"Listen Auntie Mildred I have a lot of love and respect for you, I love you like my own Auntie, but I don't appreciate you judging me like you don't have skeletons in your own closet. You think I don't smell the cigarette smoke when I walk in the door? And on Prezden's belongings from time to time when I come pick him up? And we both know you aint even supposed to be doing anything like that especially when there is oxygen in the room. So since we are having a Q & A why don't you start by telling the truth about that?"

"Yeah I might have a smoke or two from time to time, but I would never put that baby in jeopardy. Whatever I do is not right underneath him and that's for sure. But Mae Mae you are getting defensive over something that you know will take you all the way back down to the bottom. You're young and have so much ahead of you. Me I'm just an old woman basically biding my time. What happens when them boys get out of jail? That's one problem solved and another right back on the list. Look at this boy don't you think he deserves a fighting chance of having a good life? I've heard you say that yourself."

"Well Aunt Mildred I haven't said I was doing anything."

"So are you saying that you're not?"

Mae Mae burst out crying.

"It's so hard dealing with this situation that you're hard head nephew put me in. I have been strong all along, going to work, taking care of him, running back and forth to that Devil's Island. They messing with me down at the job, my best friend is out of the country right now, I have no one to talk to, I just feel so alone and it's hard trying to do this all by myself."

"Well Mae Mae what about Ms. Green have you been in contact with her? She seems to be someone who can help you and I can tell she really cares."

"I know but I just don't wanna let her down. I don't do it all the time and I feel I have it under control. Just please don't tell Jean, I can't risk Trevor finding out."

"Baby girl, you gonna have to be better than this. I know sometimes in life problems sneak up on you, but you're using them drugs to fill a void in your life and it's gonna take control of you. You haven't really been keeping up with yourself lately, you picking this baby up later and later, you been moody lately and don't think I forgot you didn't bring me back my change from the store last week. Now what would V feel about this? She really didn't want to leave on vacation from the beginning, but you convinced her that you were fine. Since she's been gone I started noticing certain changes in you. That would just kill that girl because she loves you so much. You may not have much but you have more than some and I want you to move forward in your life not backwards. You keep Trevor on his p's and q's so what happens if you fall to? What's gonna happen to this precious little baby boy?"

"Auntie you right, I'm gonna stop this now. I'm sorry if I was so

defensive with you. You mean the world to me and right now you're all that I have. I'm not trying to be hypocritical but the thought of you lighting a cigarette in this place scares the living daylights out of me. It's dangerous to the highest degree. Promise me you won't light them cancer sticks anymore and I will take everything you just said to me into consideration and I'll leave that dog food alone."

"Dog food, Mae Mae what you talking about?"

"Oh sorry, that's just another name for heroin."

"Well whatever it's called, you have to leave it alone."

"I am, I appreciate this talk and all the help you give to me.

Mae Mae and Prezden go home and she continued her nightly routine after getting Prezden to bed. She would sit in the middle of the floor flipping thru photo albums of her and Trevor, different life events, old family photos. She really started missing her family a lot. She wanted to reach out to her Mother and Father and make peace with them. Depression really started taking over. She took a liking to Yoko Ono's music as well and she would play a lot of songs from Ono's album "Seasons of Glass" basically every night. She would constantly play, I don't know why, even when you're far away and when she was in a particular mood she would keep dog town on constant repeat.

One day she got up the courage to pay her parents a visit. She arrived only to find out that her Dad had passed away 6 months prior and her Mom still wanted nothing to do with her. Her Mother wouldn't even look at Prezden as they stood at the door. Her mother shouted out in her native language mwen pa gen petit fi" which means "I have no daughter "as she slammed the door in her in Prezden's face. That drove Mae Mae over the edge. She grabbed Prezden and stormed off crying with him in her arms. Over the next few days she didn't go to work. She slipped into a deeper depression. She missed several visits up at the jail. She would not answer anyone's phone calls. She basically had everyone worried. When Jean spoke to Mildred she could not hold it in any longer and she told him that Mae Mae started back getting high again.

CHAPTER TEN

Jean was very upset and he knew that he had to tell Trevor what was going on. This couldn't have happened at a worse time. Things were looking up for he and Trevor, they were getting closer to their goal of getting their bail money and were making big plans. Jean waited a couple of days to break the news to Trevor. One afternoon Trevor and Jean were in the rec yard pumping iron and Trevor was really upset at the fact that Mae Mae had been ditching his calls and hasn't been up there to visit him in a few days. Jean told him about what was going on. Trevor broke out in an uncontrollable coughing spell and started coughing up blood. He had to be rushed to the infirmary. As Trevor lie there waiting to be treated he began coughing up blood once again. His last gurgle was heard by another inmate who was lying next to him recovering from an attempted suicide as he took his last breath choking on his own blood. Sad to say he never made it out alive.

Jean could not believe the news when he heard that his cousin didn't make it. Daniels was the one to convey the news to him. He was actually teary eyed himself as he passed the news of Trevor's death to him. Jean was at a loss for words and he went off the deep end. He was granted permission to go down to the infirmary to see him for the final time. He broke down and cried so hard, the nurse had to give him a sedative to calm him down. Trevor was a heavy smoker especially during his time of incarceration. He had Jean worried a lot lately because he started noticing signs of him not being well. But he never imagined the outcome to be anything close to this.

The next morning Jean had to make the worse phone call he would ever have to make in his entire life. He called Mae Mae and broke the unshakeable news to her. Mae Mae went completely off the deep end. Her screams were so loud and gut wrenching they could be heard by passerby's on the street. The news had spread so quickly that before she knew it she had friends and whoever she considered family knocking on her front door. Everyone was understandably upset and sympathetic towards her and the unfortunate situation. Veronica happened to call her because she was flying back in from Brazil that very afternoon when she received the unbearable news. The arrangements had to be made and a funeral service was eventually held at Armstrong Funeral home in Brooklyn. Daniels attended the service and at the end of the service he approached Mae Mae with a letter found in Trevor's belongings that he had written to her during the time he couldn't reach her.

After the service Mae Mae returned home, later that night she decided to read the letter. The letter read:

My dearest Mae Mae, I am out of my mind with worry. I don't know why I haven't heard from you or seen you. I don't know what else I could have possibly done to make you do things this way. I know I'm a fuck up, but damn don't get a nigga back like this. You are my world and you are what keeps me going.

Without you I am nothing and I have nothing. The last time you were here you said you feel like you're losing me every time you leave this place, well now I feel like I've lost you since you left

this place. Please don't give up on me now. There are some things I haven't told you, but I wanted to surprise you.

I'm only one check away from having my bail money and at least I will be out and we can begin to live life again outside these walls. Me and Jean have been doing our thing up in here, working on kitchen duty and baby I'm almost there. I can just see your whole face light up right now as you read this because that's my girl.

When I come home, I'm gonna start living a healthier life, so I can be there to watch Prezden grow up and become a better man than his old man. I guess you can say I'm in rehab now because since I've been here I haven't been getting high and I feel so clean. I mean other than these cigarettes that I plan to give up on to but hey one thing at a time. I know you're mad at me about something, but we can talk about it. If I don't hear from you soon or see you soon I'm really gonna need that 7:30 exam we talked about because I am definitely gonna lose my mind.

I will call you and hopefully I will speak to you or see you even before this letter hits the doorstep. Give Prezden a kiss for me and tell him that I love him and I love you Mrs. Dubois. You can't leave a nigga like that especially after I done took on your last name. I'm your nigga for life.

What Trevor is referring to in the letter is the fact that when he and Mae Mae had gotten married, instead of her taking on his last name which is Mitchell, they did the untraditional thing and he took on her last name. She figured that since she was disconnected from her family, and she had no siblings she still wanted to carry on the family name and Trevor honored that. She just could not stop crying and blaming herself for shutting him out during that time. She was going thru a lot, Mildred had called her out on getting high, and she had recently found out that her Dad passed away before she could even try to make things right between them. Her Mom still didn't accept her, she got fired from the supermarket from not going to work, her husband was locked up and she was raising her baby all by herself.

Veronica stayed with her day and night, never leaving her side. She took care of Prezden easing some of the pressure off of her. It seemed like no matter what Veronica or anyone did to try and help ease her pain things just continued to go downhill. She end up having a nervous breakdown and was admitted into Bellevue Hospital for mental evaluation. Veronica took custody of Prezden during this time. Jean was finally released on bail, he would go and visit Mae Mae and make sure she was being taken care of. Jean and Mildred end up moving into Mae Mae and Trevor's house since it wasn't being occupied. He kept close contact with Veronica as well.

CHAPTER ELEVEN

Meanwhile back at the prison a lot of chaos started to erupt. A lot of the jailers didn't take Trevor's death lightly; some even commented that the medical disregard in the jail was killing prisoners. They even nicknamed him Marlboro man, because most of the time when you saw him, he had a cigarette in hand or in his mouth. He was definitely missed by his clients in protective custody. What he did for them they considered good and they reaped the benefits of his comings and goings. Some missed him and some missed what he would supply to them on a daily. So much that rumors began to spread. That same prisoner named Ronnie who originally was in the cell with Trevor that Daniels had a run in with began to talk. He started complaining that Daniels showed favoritism towards Trevor because he was participating in kickback schemes with him.

He even went as far to report this to the higher ups. When Daniels found out about it he decided to do something about it and take matters into his own hands once again. In the middle of the night, he took him out of his cell and down to the TV room, where he took off his duty firearm after telling him he was tired of Ronnie being a cell warrior and made him fight him like a man. There were other guards who stood by and watched and after it was over they helped him by keeping the fight under the wraps.. This by no means stopped

Ronnie from snitching. He reported the fight and got other inmates to turn on Daniels. A full investigation was ordered. Ronnie managed to get some of the inmates to rat but others honored the code of silence. Daniels was suspended pending the investigation under alleged employee misconduct. If convicted he faces up to 6 years in prison under protective custody. There seemed to be a domino effect of pure madness following Trevor's death.

Mae Mae end up dying of a drug overdose while in the mental institution and nobody knows how she even managed to get her hands on some drugs while she was there. Aunt Mildred was flustered from one bad news after another, she went into the bathroom one day after Jean left the house and lit a cigarette with the oxygen tank by her side and it blew up causing her untimely death. Jean's case finally went to trial and he was sentenced 25 years to life for manslaughter in the 1st degree. He basically had all charges pinned on him since Trevor's role in the killing no longer made a difference. Veronica continued to take on full responsibility for Prezden over the next couple of years. Until she took ill and was diagnosed with AIDS a disease that a lot people thought at the time only affected gay men, she was no longer capable of caring for him.

Since all of the key people in Prezden's life were no longer around she made the heart breaking decision to drop him off at the front stairs of a church with a letter, some pictures and sentimental things to have him remember his family by. She rang the bell and in a slapdash fashion disappeared into the crowded streets. This would be the last time she would ever see him and she passed away eight months later.

PREZDEN

CHAPTER TWELVE

Prezden was only 5 and much too young to understand the circumstances that would soon change the rest of his life. He spent a huge portion of his younger years in and out of different foster homes, taking on abuse and neglect. He was living with a foster family in Harlem when he began kindergarten. The other children would make fun of him because of his outdated clothing and worn out haircuts. Although the children made fun of him, there was one kid named Savius that in no way treated him any different. He and Prezden would sit together at lunchtime; play in the yard and talk. Prezden and Savius continued their friendship each being assigned to the same class over the next years and they became best friends.

When Prezden turned 8 he was adopted by a wealthy middle aged couple Mr. & Mrs. Valentine. Mrs. Valentine was an anesthesiologist at Harlem Hospital and Mr. Valentine was an Architect and part owner of an architectural firm he founded.

The Valentine's tried for many years to have children but each time, turning up fruitless. They were determined that one day their love and devotion would occupy a young person's life. They both saw something special in Prezden and were prepared to provide him a bright and capable future. They treated him as if he were they're natural born child despite differences in race. Prezden was thrilled about his new parents and new home but was saddened by the thought of being separated from Savius. He tried to masquerade his feelings as much as possible because he didn't want to disappoint them and he feared being sent back in the system. It didn't take long for them to realize that something was bothering him, so they sat him down letting him know that it was okay for him to express whatever was on his mind. Prezden explained that he really didn't want to switch schools and he feared losing that close contact with his only friend. They immediately understood the situation and took in consideration all of the losses he experienced early on so they arranged for him to continue his schooling in Harlem. Prezden would have weekly visits with a child psychiatrist to smooth the progress of him regaining balance in his life.

As the years went on he grew very close to the Valentines even calling them Mom and Dad. With all the love they gave to him and the counseling, he learned to accept the here and now to a large degree. Savius and Prezden's friendship remained unchanged. They both graduated from the 6th grade and moved on to the same Junior High School. Savius lived in the projects, being raised by his Mother alone. He never really knew his father who was extradited back to Panama for reproduction of counterfeit money. Savius and his Mother, Ms. Lexington, kept an airtight Mother to Son relationship. Ms. Lexington struggled to make ends meet, keeping a roof over their head and food on the table.

She provided child care to the neighborhood children and she also did housekeeping on the weekends. Savius watched his mother struggle for so many years that he vowed to one day make more than enough money to provide his mother the type of comfortable life he felt she deserved. Everyone in the neighborhood knew Ms. Lexington and shared a great amount of respect for her. They even nick named her Miss. Lexy. Savius and Prezden discovered that they had a number of things in common. Neither one of them ever really knew their fathers, they had no siblings and they experienced ups and downs in their early childhood. As the years went by the two would unleash different problems and situations in their lifetime which strengthened their link which was more like brothers from a different mother as they would refer to one another.

They spent significant time at each other's homes. Savius loved the fact that Prezden lived in a house with a swimming pool in the backyard. And a court height basketball hoop. They would play basketball in the yard for hours. Mrs. Valentine would wait on them hand and foot, serving them anything from an ice cold glass of lemonade to their favorite foods. She also kept an easel in the yard and would spend time in between painting. She was a very talented painter but she kept is as a hobby. Mr. Valentine would spend time playing chess with his close friend and business partner Darnell, or reading the newspaper, readers digest architectural digest, national geographic and Time Magazines.

One day he was reading an article in the Time Magazine about a young boy Ronnie "Yummy" Sandifer. According to the article, he lived a short violent life and he was so young to kill and so young to die. He led a violent street life and eventually died the same way. Mr. Valentine showed Prez the article and had him read it. This was his subtle way of reminding him that no matter how much you may love the streets, the streets don't love you back.

As mentioned before the Valentines were open to allowing Prez to spend time at Savius house but they started noticing certain changes in Prez. They would have these heated discussions at times because Mrs. Valentine basically accepted the changes as growing pangs and the natural differences in their cultures. Mr. Valentine didn't agree. He would have these conversations with Darnell from time to time and Darnell would advise him to keep a close eye on Prez because he's heard a lot about the things that go on in that neighborhood. The Valentines did a lot for Prez in terms of keeping him knowledgeable on different things in life. They traveled many places such as The National Great Blacks Museum in Baltimore Maryland, camping at Martha's Vineyard, bringing Savius along They took Prezden to food tasting events, getting him familiar with different cultures. They went to different amusement parks such as Great Adventure and Kings Dominion, the Bronx Zoo, they vacationed in Puerto Rico, London and Canada you name it.

Although, Prezden had exposure to these different experiences, he still hungered for the enjoyment of visiting Savius because he had an excitement about the projects and he also had a big heart for a girl named Khandi. She was intelligent, funny, and very attractive and she had a broad sense for fashion. She was used to having the finer things in life. She went to an all-girls private school just blocks away from home on the upper east side of Manhattan. The building she lived in had a full time doorman, 24-hour concierge, and just steps away from Central Park, close to shopping, dining and museums. She lived a stylish and comfortable life but when her parents separated she and her mother moved in with her Grandmother, Ms. Anne. Ms. Anne lived in the building right next to Savius. Kenneth Kashman, Khandi's father, was an assistant manager at an Italian Restaurant named Giovanni's and her mother, Ursula Kashman, was a head wardrobe and costume designer in the film, television and theater industry.

When she found out that she was pregnant with Khandi she decided to put her professional career on standstill while Mr. Kashman took on more hours at the restaurant and completed his college education obtaining his degree in business management. He eventually accepted an offer to become manager at a very lucrative Mercedes Benz dealership making a very attractive salary. He networked with a large number of people and exchanged different ideas, especially at these social events held at his boss's home. Even though the money he made was good, he still wanted more. There was a lot of temptation which developed into greed. He flew down to Atlanta one weekend on a business trip and ran into one of his former college buddy named Frank Booker.

Frank was one of those people who felt college was really a waste of time so he ended up dropping out. He believed in instant achievement. He started countless hustles to make a living. He was able to reach certain goals, such as purchasing two high end foreign vehicles, one vacation home in Jamaica and a luxurious condo in Atlanta and not to mention he was a very flashy and expensive dresser. Although, Frank accomplished certain things, his hustle was never steady. He experienced his highs and lows but he was a painless talker and quick thinker. When he and Kenneth met up needless to say that he was at one of his lows. He made Kenneth an offer to go into business with him, stealing cars from the dealership and sell them overseas making an untraceable large amount of money. He put together a plan that would go down over the next six months. Kashman was reluctant at first but it didn't take much time before he accepted the deal which ruined his life in the next two years and many more to come.

When shit hit the fan he was under investigation he and Frank were both arrested. He quickly was able to make bail while awaiting trial. Mrs. Kashman couldn't undertake the pressure of the feds sitting outside the apartment, watching their every move. They even followed her and Khandi wherever they would go. The worse part about this is that she was totally innocent and had no knowledge of her husband's corrupt dealings. Things started to go downhill between her and her husband. He denied the accusations but she started to have suspicions that he was not telling her the truth and this put a real strain on their relationship. He was found guilty and had very little time to spend with his family before his scheduled sentencing. The last Friday that he spent with Khandi and her mother he got dressed to go to the store to bring Khandi back her favorite chocolate ice cream on a sugar cone as a token of his love from him to her, but he never returned. Since then she detested chocolate ice cream, sugar cones and any constructive thoughts of her Father.

Ms. Lexy would take care of Khandi after school she and Savius friendship became tighter and tighter. They treated each other like brother and sister. Prezden had a crush on Khandi from the very first time he ever laid eyes on her. For a long time he kept his sentiment for Khandi on mute because he wasn't confident that the feelings would be mutual. So he would just act natural whenever she was around. He felt that with a well put together girl like Khandi he needed to have his shit up to the mark.

Over time he learned that Khandi was a simple, down to earth type of girl with a lot of class about herself and a beauty that came from the inside out. When it was time for high school, Prez, Savius and Khandi were all accepted to Julia Richmond. It was at this time that Prez's interactions with Khandi became more personal. He and Savius joined the basketball team and Khandi was on the cheerleading squad. Prezden and Khandi would talk a lot on the bus whenever there were away from home games.

They exchanged telephone numbers and would spend hours talking on the phone about any and everything. They gained a strong connection as time went on. Their bond had really gotten tighter once Khandi found out that her mother's battle with breast cancer had taken a turn for the worse. She was hospitalized at Memorial Sloan Kettering located only a block away from their High School. Prezden would go with Khandi to visit her on a daily basis. All the way up until the day she passed away.

Khandi watched her mother do everything to live a clean and healthy life in spite of the breast cancer. She ate right, she worked out, took all her vitamins and she even kept steady appointments with a holistic doctor. Although the loss was great, Ursula was always a very religious and spiritual person and she raised Khandi to be the same way. She was very thankful to still have her Grandmother in her life.

Khandi drew closer to Prezden at this time and he decided that he really needed to step things up because he absolutely adored the way Khandi would make him feel needed and she wanted him in her life now more than ever. This made him feel more like a man and he loved that feeling and was ready to do anything to keep the feelings growing.

During these High School years Prez and Savius became cool with a few of their teammates and Khandi became cool with a few girls on the cheerleading squad. There was Solomon, Roof, Raze, Swift, Kizma, Chloe, Terri and Donna. Donna and Khandi were very close and became best friends. They all managed to merge together and become a tight little family unit.

They would do a lot of group things, like get together and go skating at Skate Key in the Bronx; they would go to the movies at Whitestone in the Bronx or down on 42nd street, they would go out to eat at Sylvia's , Sherman's , Jackson hole for the Jumbo burgers. They would pack up for the day and hit Coney Island. Khandi would be so eager because she really loved the cotton candy and the Nathan's hot dogs.

One weekend they all got together to watch a new movie coming out called Scream. After the movie they were on the way home, traveling on the A train and Roof kept running up on people quoting a line from the movie. "What's your favorite scary movie" and he would laugh hysterically because of the surprised reactions he would get from certain people.

He ran up on this one man while he was reading the newspaper and the man hardly found anything to be funny. He was so startled that he jumped and the newspaper went flying out of his hands and papers went soaring in all directions. The man got so mad that he punched Roof in the face sending him sailing two poles down causing his head to hit the end door that separates the cars.

The girls started screaming as the man went charging at Roof for some more. Prezden jumped in front to intervene and he was trying to apologize to the man for Roof's behavior. The man just kept going with the enraged anger and he pushed Prez up against the pole. Prez and the man started fighting. Prez hit the man so hard that he knocked two of his front teeth right out the socket, leaving one imbedded in his knuckle. Blood was everywhere.

They saw there was a transit cop the next car over and he was quickly making his way to the car that they were in. The train stopped on 125th street and the group darted off the train safely making it off the platform vanishing into the congested streets escaping any repercussions from the law. It seemed like almost every time they would go out on group outings something was bound to go wrong one way or another.

There was another incident when they went to see the movie set it off and this time Swift kept talking throughout the movie and he got into an altercation with 3 guys that shouted out telling him to shut the fuck up. Swift threw his popcorn at them and a fight broke out. It end up turning into a brawl and they were thrown out the theater. After a string of incidents Khandi and Prez decided to do a lot of the double dating thing with Donna and her boyfriend Chuck. Chuck didn't attend the same High School; he went to the Bronx High School of Science. He was 2 years older and he was steps ahead with graduating. Chuck was more of a brainy laid back type of dude that basically goes with the flow. Donna was more of the outgoing, kind of loud and very opinionated type of person. This was a classic case of opposites attracting. Donna met him at a science fair and they got to talking and cliqued from that point on.

When Khandi and Prez would double date with Donna and Chuck, they did different things like going to the Museum of

Natural History, The Botanical Gardens in Brooklyn, The New York Aquarium, they would walk around Chelsea Piers, have picnics in Central Park and they spent a lot of quality time. Chuck's Favorite restaurant was Delmonico's. He's been going there since he was a child with his parents and three little sisters Triseama, Marquee and Monet. He impressed Donna by taking her there on their very first date and they introduced it to Khandi and Prez. It was a bit pricey so they would plan for it and they would go to Delmonico's at least once every other month.

CHAPTER THIRTEEN

Although, Prezden was living a pretty good life with the Valentines he still had a thirst for wealth along with authority and respect. He and Savius would sit on the project benches, watch and listen to the big hustlers run game getting paid from all the ill-gotten gains. They drove swanky whips and wore up to the minute designer clothing and jewelry. Prezden called it doing his math and here's how he explained it to Savius.

"First we get on the right side of them old gee's, then we estimate, subtract them add ourselves, sum it all up then begin to multiply. We would just be picking up where they leave off."

Prezden was more of the officious type and Savius was the laid back in the cut type of guy, but they were both ready to do whatever , by any means necessary to fast lane their continued existence of the average everyday life they were living compared to the advanced few. The key player of the pack was named Major. Major had control, dominance and clout in his area of play. There were a handful that hungered for the opportunity to seize power from Major, but no one had the moral fiber to blaze that trail. Major lived with his father up until the early portion of his teenage years.

He couldn't withstand the abuse brought on by his father. Nothing he would do ever materialize to be up to standard in his father's eyes. He would verbally abuse him, calling him names like, stupid, worthless and that he would never amount to anything. Cheerless to say that his mother met her maker immediately following his birth and his father railed against him from day one as a result. Although people would tell him that could never be true, it was on many occasions confirmed by the things he would say to him.

He reminded him damn near every day that if his mother would have listened and had an abortion, she would still be here. He was faced with what seemed like never ending physical abuse from his father as well. If Major was ten minutes late coming home from school his father would be standing by the door and he would go upside his head with his fist. If he didn't have things in rank around the house he would get smacked and punched around.

One night Major fell asleep rather than ironing his clothes for school and his father's uniform for work. His father woke him up in the middle of the night shouting and screaming all types of profanity. He turned on the iron and burned him on his back as he was walking away. The next couple of days when he went to school he pressed the issue to change in the locker room for gym and it sent a signal to his teacher that something was wrong. He eventually showed the burn to his gym teacher and authorities were notified and he was removed from the household. He eventually was returned back to the home to live with his father after his father convinced the authorities that it was an accident.

He ran away from home so many times and while on the streets he would get into all sorts of trouble. His father saw him as a problem bigger than he was willing to solve and had him placed in a group home. Major grew up with an attitude that was tough as old boots. After breaking a few noses, knocking out a few of the finest and ruining their reputations, he started making his money and he gained much respect.

When it came to Prez he felt they had a lot in common. Major saw Prez as his mirror image. He would hit Prez up with his quick witted street smarts nearly on a daily basis. Prez would find time to make routine stops to visit Major that remained uninterrupted and this is what Major was most impressed by and his strong feelings to earn the mean green.

Savius would go all out for his love for basketball to a great extent. He aimed at this possibly being his ticket to the well to do life he always yearned for. On the other side of things Prez was more to the point of feeding his hunger by dealing big business becoming a high roller earning ready money. Savius didn't hang around Major as much because he felt they were being taken for granted. He would tell Prez that they were hostages to fortune Major would do things like send them to the warehouse, which was the place where he stored all the goods, anything from ammunition, to money and drugs. The warehouse was located in Mr. D's basement.

Mr. D was an old timer who ran a little newspaper stand selling all kinds of things like candy, gum, soda, juice, coffee, tea, magazines and cigarettes. This was his little business that kept him busy and away from the eyes of the law. He was a big time number runner back in the day and it was said that he used to be a trigger man but that was never really confirmed. He still ran numbers from the spot but on a much lower scale.

However, he knows a lot about how shit go in the streets so he looked out for Major and allowed him to set up shop and taught him the ropes on how to do his street business but also how to stay out of trouble. He also told him never sit on dirty work too long. Create something for yourself so you don't have to chase the streets for the rest of your life. He's seen too many end up dead, in jail, or rejects because the street game changes all the time. He called it build and destroy. He told Major the only sure way to success is to establish, build and pass off. He kept Major informed on a lot of things he felt he should know. He once told Major that he learned a lot of what he knows from talking to a wise fool. When asked what he meant he explained it as "A wise man feels he knows it all by study and research, but a wise fool knows what he knows by experience. Mr. D was real cool with a lot of people including some crooked cops and a few retired judges so he was secure in his spot.

Major would send Savius and Prez over there to pick up or drop off and hit them off with spending cash that Savius would refer to as pocket change. Prez didn't really care about the money; he paid more attention of the details of the operation. What they both didn't realize was that in the beginning they were being put to the test, the true test. Major would send them on dummy runs. They would think they were picking up weed and it was really crushed green tea leaves. They would think they were picking up coke and it was really bags of baking soda. They would think they were picking up ammunition which was really movie prop guns that Major stole years ago backstage at a play he went to see with the counselors from the group home.

This went about a month before he actually started sending them back and forth with the real deal. Major would split them up and give them different jobs just to see if he can trust one without the other. Prez always looked at is as treading water. When asked what he meant by this, he explained it to Savius like this.

"When you first learn how to swim every beginner must learn how to stay safe around the water right? And how do you do that? By treading water. So treading is the most important skill needed after taking that plunge if the water is over your head."

"While these dudes do the plunging we keep our heads above water and observe watching some sink or swim. So I'll keep treading until I get that lucky shot at that assignment with more responsibility and prove myself to Major and then some."

Prezden was a careful observer and deep thinker, he believed that

patience, effort and dedication can get him just about anything he wanted or needed in due time.

CHAPTER FOURTEEN

Prezden found a way to balance school, home, his relationship with Khandi and his attachment with Major. Major was planning to relocate by the end of next year. He brought a house in Philadelphia for him, his girlfriend Tiara and little daughter Cadena. He also took Mr. D's advice and he purchased property and it was under renovation. He was in the process of obtaining his tobacco and liquor license. Once the renovation is complete it's going to be a Cigar bar, with a huge Humidor filled with a vast collection of some of the best cigars from around the world, a stage for a live band, a back room with a couple of chess/checker tables and a bar fully stocked with some of the best beers, rums, whiskey's, scotch's and wines. Major had it all planned out and on the weekends he would go out to Philly and leave Prez in charge of things around the way. This was that Lucky break Prez was looking forward to.

The Valentines were planning a ten day vacation to Tahiti for their 30th wedding anniversary, so Prez wanted to do something nice for them before they leave. He and Khandi put their money together and set up a dinner date at Wo Hop's in Chinatown. This gave Khandi an opportunity to get to know the Valentines even better. Prezden brought his mom a bouquet of Peruvian Lilies. He pulled two single ones from the bouquet, pulling Khandi's hair to one side placing one of the flowers on the side of her hair. Mrs. Valentines happened to catch of glimpse of the earrings Khandi was wearing.

"Khandi are those Tahitian black Pearls in your ear?"

"Yes they are Tahitian south sea Pearl & diamond hoops that once belonged to my mother."

"Your Mom was a woman of good taste I can see, they are absolutely lovely."

"Thank you, I would only wear them on special occasions and today is definitely a special occasion."

Mr. Valentine interjects by making a throat clearing sound hinting Mrs. Valentine's attention. She realized that he wanted her to mention the anniversary gift he brought for her.

"Oh by the way speaking of pearls this is my gift from Mr. Valentine." She drew back her sweater collar displaying her black pearl necklace.

"I love it, it's very beautiful, let me guess Tahitian?"

"It most certainly is Khandi. Tahitian pearls are the only natural
black pearls in the world. All other saltwater and freshwater pearls must be dyed in order to achieve that color."

"Hmmm…. interesting. So speaking of Tahiti Prez tells me that you guys will be vacationing there in the next few days?"

"Yes we are and I am so excited, my husband is just full of goodies, we'll be catching the red eye on Wednesday and we'll be returning in two weeks on Wednesday the 27th."

"You guys are lucky to get away from this cold weather at least for a little while. Where only into the third week of winter and already I can't wait for the summer."

"Ma, what did you get dad for your anniversary?"

"While you were playing basketball and your father was busy playing chess, I've been full of activity myself, painting a portrait of your father and I. I copied it from a picture we took years ago and it came out perfect."

They ate, talked, laughed and had a really good time. They discussed future plans for education and career goals. Khandi and Prez talked a lot about one day opening a barber/beauty shop. Prez was preparing to go to barber school and Khandi was preparing to go to school for cosmetology in September. The valentine's supported him in his decision and dreams although if they had it their way they would prefer him to go off to college and get a degree. Savius was offered a full basketball scholarship at Boston College and was leaving in September. This would be the first time he and Prez would be separated.

The Valentines had made prior arrangements with Ms. Lexi, allowing Prez to stay with her and Savius during the time that they would be away. That Wednesday the Valentine's boarded their red eye flight from JFK Airport. The Valentine's kept in contact with Prez checking in to make sure everything was good with him. Although Prez was chilling and doing a lot more in the streets with them being gone, he still missed them.

The night the Valentines were due to return home, Prez was at Khandi's house watching the 24th American Music Awards. Khandi was so happy and shouting for joy when Toni Braxton won for favorite soul/R&B artist and Favorite soul/R&B album Secrets. She ran to the phone and called Donna and they immediately started talking about the breath taking dress Toni was wearing that night as she received her award and was giving her acceptance speech. They went on to compare notes about the show as a whole, like who was wearing what, who they felt should have won and who they felt shouldn't have. They were so busy talking that Khandi kept ignoring a repeated call coming in on the other line. She finally answered and it was bad news.

The Valentine's boarded their flight leaving from Tahiti, but tragedy struck and they would never make it home. The aircraft crashed during takeoff killing the pilot, ten other passengers and themselves. This accident was called one of the worse in the area in current years. Prez was devastated; lost and confused. He had already experienced a lot of losses in his life and could never contemplate something like this happening. He had gotten used to having a stable family household.

He was graduating from high school in June. He really started learning the ropes on how the business ran down there with Major. His promising future suddenly turned into the darkest of days. Khandi and Savius were by his side night and day. Prez was only 17 at the time and was still considered a minor. Going back into the system was not an option for him. Mrs. Valentine was survived by her brother Richard who lived in Maine and Mr. Valentine was survived by a sister named Carol who lived in Tennessee. They didn't see each other much giving the distance they lived and would see each other occasionally on holidays over the years but their main source of contact was over the phone, so Prez was never that close with either one of them. Ms. Lexi was always like a second mother to him and she insisted that he come live with her and Savius.

CHAPTER FIFTEEN

The Valentines had a life insurance policy and a will. Before leaving for Tahiti they met with their lawyer and made some changes to their will. They were always very detailed people who thought ahead for the future. It was almost like they were preparing for the worse and knew they weren't coming back. In the will they named Darnell as their personal representative, naming him the main person to follow the instructions given in the will.

He helped Prez to locate all of the paperwork and took the initiative to help in planning the funeral. Since Mr. Valentine had served time in the military in his youthful years, he and his wife were both buried in a military cemetery in NY. Darnell was still in the process of paying off any and all debts that the Valentines had. This included medical bills, funeral, credit cards, the mortgage and taxes. Once all business was squared away, the house they lived in and Mr. Valentine's portion of the business he and Darnell were partnered in was left to Carol and Richard. They eventually sold the property, allowed Darnell to buy them out of their inherited portion of the business and split the profits Prez was left with a healthy lump sum of money but the funds were held in a special account.

Between the life insurance policies, and family inheritance, pensions, 401k after all obligations were squared off he was left with $3,000,000.00 dollars. This was set up in a trust payable over a 10 year period. So his first check would be in the amount of $300,000.00, and he would receive his first payment when he turns 19 years old.

Months go by and it's June. Prez, Khandi and Savius graduate High School. It's been five months since the Valentines had passed away. Prez has not gotten over the hurt and pain of losing them, but it's become a little easier to deal with. Khandi, Savius and Major were his biggest rocks holding him down and supporting him during these dark days. They spent a lot of time together over the summer. Major wanted to do something nice for Prez and keep his mind off things so the day after graduation Major flew Prez and Savius with him to the MGM Grand Garden Arena in Las Vegas to watch the Tyson vs. Holyfield fight.

This fight was one that went down in history after Tyson bit a chunk out of Holyfield's ear and spit it into the mat, turning the crowd into absolute pandemonium. They spent the night down in Las Vegas and returned the following Sunday night. Khandi was a little disappointed because she kind of felt left out. Prez explained that it was a boys thing and that at the end of the summer before they all start their schooling in Sept. they are planning to go to the Budweiser super fest tour in Philadelphia to see the performances of Mary J. Blige, Aaliyah, Ginuwine, Bone Thugs–N-Harmony and Dru Hill.

Since Savius was leaving in September for School. Ms. Lexi put

together a care package for him that consisted of the basic necessities like toothpaste, soap, lotion, towels, washcloths, slippers, t-shirts underwear, socks, a winter coat, and few other things. Savius appreciated it and he knew that Ms. Lexi would make a big fuss over it if he would have tried stopping her. He purchased all of his personal get fly stuff because he wanted to be on point when he got to Boston, so he pushed a lot of work with Prez and Major to get up more than enough to make it happen. He brought 2 pair of Jordan's, 2 throwback Jerseys, a couple of polo shirts, 3 pairs of Polo jeans, 2 Nautica sweatshirts, a pair of DKNY boots, 1 Enyce sweater and 2 Ecko Unlimited hoodies. Khandi brought him a Coogi sweater.

They hit up the Versace store on 5th avenue. Savius brought 2 pair of jeans, a belt, cologne, and 2 long sleeve button ups. A week after shopping at Versace on 5th Ave it was reported on the news that Versace was shot to death and killed at his front gate by Andrew Cunanan. The prices of Versace's line sudden skyrocketed.

Weeks go by and summer is about to end. Ms. Anne had spoken to Major's girlfriend Tiara and she agreed to let Khandi stay in Philly at their house along with Prez and Savius so they can all go to the Budweiser Super fest. Ms. Anne knew Tiara very well; she watched her grow so she was comfortable and trusted that Khandi would be fine. Ms. Lexi was fine with it as well; she knew that when the boys were with Major they were in good hands.

Khandi really wished that Donna could be there, but she was down in North Carolina at her family reunion and wasn't coming back until after Labor Day. This was the first time they ever been to Philly and they would finally get the chance to see Major's house that he so proudly spoke about. They were so fascinated at the layout and how it was stylishly decorated. The guys spent time watching sports on the 55" inch Sony Projection television, listening to music and playing a couple hands of poker down in the basement.

Khandi spent time talking with Tiara and playing with their little daughter Cadena. Prez made a promise to Khandi that one day they will get a dope house together and have it laid out with all the finer things he knew she deserved and have her sitting like a queen on her throne. Khandi always had faith in Prez and she never doubted any promises he ever made. Prez was always a go getter and his word was solid as gold. He was always determined and would make things happen in due time. They went to the concert the next day. All performers rocked Khandi's favorite was Mary and Aaliyah. Prez and Savius was up on Bone Thugz-N-Harmony. Over all they had a blast.

The following week Savius left for Boston. Khandi started Cosmetology school, Prez began Barber School and Donna started her first semester at BMCC. Things were going according to plan. Prez continued to watch over things for Major on the weekends. Every Wednesday he would hold things down while Major would go to the chess and checker house down in Central park and compete with "the old heads." a term Major says he picked up in Philly.

Prez would finish barber school in 5 1/2 months. He graduated the second week in February. By the first week in March he rented a booth at Kaseam's barber shop and began putting his cutting skills to the test. All of his friends would come in to get a fresh cut and hang around a bit talking shit. He worked in the shop a couple of hours in the mornings and continued his work with Major.

Major finally got his business up and running and threw a launch party in June. He and Prez had a long talk about things. He told Prez that he would need him to put more time in because he wasn't gonna be around as much. Prez cut the days in half and only worked at the shop three days a week out of loyalty to Major.

The other four days of the week he put his boy Caesar on letting him use the space He was a cool dude and he had good cutting skills as well. Savius was home from school for the summer he stepped up and put in hours with Prez.

Khandi was still in cosmetology school and on the weekends she and her classmate Cheray worked at Destiny's hair salon washing hair just to get that experience of being in a real salon outside of school. This was the first summer that the group didn't spend that much time going out and doing fun shit. They were all busy focusing on making money and career goals. The biggest event of the summer is when Major had his Launch Party.

Everyone was in attendance. Solomon, Roof Raze, Chuck, Savius , Prez, Khandi, Khandi's classmate Cheray, Donna, Terri, Kizma, Chloe, Khandi's cousin Lisa, the Barber shop owner Kaseam, Cesar, Mr. D and many others from around the way. They rented hotel rooms and stayed in Philly for the night. Major's launch party was the talk of the town over the next few weeks. It seemed like the summer just whizzed by before you knew it September was creeping up and Savius was getting ready to go back to Boston and start a new semester.

Shortly after returning to school, he had an accident on the court. He had a bad fall, tearing his ACL and dislocating his shoulder. After receiving medical treatment, he returned home and his future basketball dreams were put on hold and so was his scholarship.

CHAPTER SIXTEEN

One Saturday afternoon Major was sitting at the stone top checker/chess tables sipping on some scotch and smoking his favorite Juan Lopez cigars and he invited Prez to join him in a game of chess.

"Yo Prez do you know how to play chess?"

"I'm not that good but my father taught me a thing or two. I know the basics of the game."

"The purpose of the game is to checkmate the opponent's king. This happens when the king is put into check and cannot get out of check. It's a done deal, checkmate game over."

"You got good enough for me young blood."

"You know you got an old head on those young shoulders, you leave a good impression. Here, have a Juan Lopez on me."

He hands Prez the cigar and Prez immediately started to jump right in and light up.

"Whoa young blood, not so quick, 1st you have to cut the cigar, place the blade where the cigar meets the wrapper, right here, now cut it with one chop. When you light up only use this kind of lighter." Reaching in his shirt pocket he pulls out a lighter.

"This is butane lighter, here keep this, I have another one in the car. Or you can use those long wooden matches; you know the kind that's used when lighting a grill."

"What's the difference?"

"Well if you use one of the two, it won't change the flavor of the cigar. Now hold the flame in front of the cigar without touching it. Now take a pull and inhale it until it's lit but don't inhale the smoke, just hold it and savor the flavor. Now let's enjoy with an alcoholic beverage, have a shot of this scotch and let's get this game started."

"Eh Major you running on a skeleton crew today, where everybody at?"

"Well today is a special kind of day, I gave everybody the day off. By the end of the game you'll understand why."

"Oh ok, I know it's for a good reason, but shit it seems weird, nobody jumping benches and hopping fences."

They begin to laugh and do a little small talk before starting their game of chess.

"Yo shit crazy out here young blood. Stay on point for real. You hear about the chinks getting robbed last night? One got shot in the face."

"I heard something about that. I heard some shit last week to, up on 125 on the west side, dude got murked stepping out a cab. Yeah the streets are hot these days."

"Yeah I hear it's them stick up kids."

"I don't know cause I hear it may be the work of a one man show."

"Either way, I got that hot lead for one or many but I'm just tryna chill. Ya heard?"

"No doubt."

You can tell Major really approves of Prez because it's very rare that he would ever share his cigars that cost close to $500.00 with only 25 in a box. Prez and Major played an intense game that lasted over an hour. The match was almost as intense as the one back in May with Garry Kasparov playing against the IBM super computer deep blue. Finally Prez called out "check mate" affirming himself the winner of the game. Although Prez won the match he was very shocked because he was definitely an armature next to Major.

Major stood up looking at Prez giving him a steady stare with that hard-edge exterior he naturally has about himself.

He says to Prez, "You know what this means right young blood?"

"What's that Major?"

"You the King now, you got my respect, you paid your dues and then some. You always stayed consistent in your pursuit of money wealth and power and you never, not once made any noisy money so now it's time to pass the baton." He digs in his pocket taking out a set of keys handing them over to Prez.

"What's this Major?"

"These are the keys to the warehouse, Mr. D already knows what's up and it's yours now young blood."

"Yo Major I don't even know what to say."

"There's nothing to say, you earned this right so just handle your business like you been doing and you'll be fine. You know all the ends and outs of how shit goes so you straight. I'm just gonna say one thing like Mr. D told me long ago. Don't get too comfortable, build and pass off."

"You will know when it's time and you won't regret it. This games changes all the time, you know what I'm talking about?"

"Also, you choose who you wanna keep on and who you wanna let go. What's Save gonna do? Is he going back to school?"

"He's still doing physical therapy, but on some real, I know Save and if it aint right and balling is over, he aint going back to Beantown."

"Save is your right hand so I know whatever it is, he gonna be good. My only suggestion right now is to check out Mateo, he's pretty much on point. Shit he has that drive like you so you might wanna keep him going when he comes back."

"When he coming back?"

"He should be back in the next couple of weeks. You know he had to take care of some bullshit that went down with Rome."

"Yeah I heard he got hemmed up fucking with the Africans down on 28th."

"I don't know the whole story but that's kind of the word on the streets. You know Mateo protective over his lil brother, so he only gonna say but so much."

"Word up. Maybe time away is what that nigga needs cause he's always getting in some shit. That nigga a real hot head, always quick to jump no matter what without thinking about shit. I think that nigga touched."

"They on some modern day Cain and Abel yo. One laid back in the cut doing his thing and the other a walking time bomb."

"That's that Milano shit far as I'm concerned know what I mean Prez? They got that black/ Italian blood mixed up in them. Anyway I told that nigga do what he gotta do. You already know, you my lil brother and I would do the same for you."

"Major man, I appreciate everything, and I'm gonna hold shit down. I got the most respect for you and I wanna say thank you." The two shake hands and give a give a thug hug.

When Mateo came back Prez decided to keep him on and working in his camp. Mateo always looked up to Major and he hoped that one day he would be next in line to take over and run shit. He was feeling a little salty that Prez was chosen instead of him. He confronted Major about it and Major put him in check and shut him down.

"Major, I thought we were good with me leaving town for a minute taking care of family business?"

"You right, so what u sayin?"

"I'm saying I leave and come back and everything! I mean this whole shit done changed. You stepped back and handed shit over to Prez, I thought I was next in order."

"Whoa! Hole up! You leaving town aint got Nathan to do with my decision. Whether you stayed, or left and came back shit was still gonna go down the same way."

"So you were never happy with my work, the way I always do things and hold things down?"

"Yo, what u think? This was some kind of race? Like I had y'all niggas running up the flagpole so I can see who salutes? Don't question my choice, matter fact any sound decisions that I make. I been in the game for a long time. I like you young buck, but this conversation right here, I'm not feeling. Instead you should see it for what it is. Prez kept you on, so you still got a spot and making money. So instead of complaining you should be thankful. Plus we talking about my lil brother right now, he got his own niggas and he didn't have to keep you on at all."

"You right, you right Major. I wasn't tryna bash your ears, I guess I was feeling guilty about not being around. I just got a lot of things on my mind. You know with Rome and shit."

"I hear you. Everything straight with that? Cause if not let a nigga know. Prez can buy you some more time."

"Yeah we straight, gotta keep pushing. I can't be missing out on my money anyway I'm tryna turn my pennies into pounds. Like you always say, can't have more money than sense."

They changed the subject of the conversation and things basically went back to normal.

Prez also recruited Swift, Roof and Raze. Savius was basically chillin on the sidelines, trying to get back to normal. He would always have a spot right next to Prez so that was never an issue. Solomon was in Atlanta living that campus life up in Spelman

College studying to be an electrical engineer. Prez had it all on lock from the start and business was running smooth.

CHAPTER SEVENTEEN

Major would visit Prez and Mr. D at least once a month. Major and Prez would call one another on a weekly basis. Prez looked up to Major like a big brother Major protected and looked after him like a little brother. Over the years they developed a bond that could not be broken.

Major was having Thanksgiving dinner at his house he invited Prez, Khandi, Savius and Donna. He left Raze in charge while away. Mateo had a problem with that because he didn't feel Raze was fit to hold it down. Prez stuck to his decision and continued on with his plans. They rode Amtrak there and back. During the train ride they talked about a lot and the topic of Prez's inheritance came up.

"Yo, when I get my doe next month I'm getting a G ride yo, brown paper bagging it straight off the lot and we riding up G style next go round, me and first lady front styling and yawl jokers slumped in the back." Laughing they relaxed and chilled the rest of the ride and Major picked them up from the station.

The day after thanksgiving the girls went black Friday shopping at The King of Prussia Mall with Tiara and Cadena.

Khandi wanted to buy something really nice for Prez since he had a birthday coming up in two weeks. She brought him a Movado watch from Neiman Marcus and a Gucci sweat suit. During their visit they spent time at Lorenzo's (Major's Cigar Lounge). They stayed in Philly over the next three days returning back to the city that Sunday morning.

Two weeks go by and it's Prez's birthday. Donna, Chuck, Khandi, Prez, Savius and Leah, a shorty Savius used to chill with when he was away at school, went to Delmonico's to celebrate. Prez was showered with gifts. Khandi had given him the watch, sweat suit and he loved it. Savius had brought him a Gucci money clip wallet. Donna brought him a bottle of Gucci Envy Cologne.

The following Monday Prez met up with the Lawyer, signed all paperwork and signed his 1st annual inheritance check in the lump sum amount of $300,000.00. He gave Ms. Lexi $20,000.00; he brought an Acura RL straight off the lot for 36K in cash. He brought Khandi a diamond engagement ring. He was already making good money doing what he does, so this was like a bonus.

Khandi completed her cosmetology course and graduated on Dec. 22nd two days before Christmas. Prez proposed to Khandi on Christmas Day. They had an engagement party on Valentine's Day at Giovanni's, the same Italian restaurant Mr. Kashmen use to manage and Mrs. Kashmen used to love dining there years ago when she was still alive. So one way or another Khandi felt a connection to this place.

Khandi accepted Prez's proposal of course, but they didn't put a rush on things. They decided that they would wait until the time was right. Before they actually tie the knot. The engagement was a way of certifying the authenticity of their relationship. Khandi started working at Destiny's beauty shop on a full time basis. Although Prez and Khandi had all intentions of opening their own beauty/barber shop they decided they would invest in buying a house first then once they get comfortable with that, they will go ahead and pursue their business opportunities.

During the time that the Valentines had passed away, Prez, Khandi, Donna and Savius were at the house cleaning and packing the stuff that Prez would keep. Prez found a box in the wall safe of the Valentines bedroom. Inside the box was all the momentous that Veronica had left in his possession the day she dropped him off at the front doors of the church. The Valentines were waiting for that ready moment in life that they felt he would be able to handle things before they would present it to him.

Although, his birth parents died so early in his childhood and he had a shaded memory of them, he now had quite a number of things to remember them by. There were pictures, a letters his Dad had written to his Mother while he was in jail. There was a five page letter Veronica had written him explaining a lot about his life, his parents and the reason she decided to give him up. She also included information about his Dad's cousin Jean who was still locked up doing a 25 to life bid.

He now had a box full of history linking him back to his past including the house he lived in with his parents in Brooklyn. Prez wrote to Jean on several occasions and he kept money on his books. Jean was way up north in the Fish Kills, so it this wouldn't be a quick little visit, Prez, Khandi and Savius made plans to go visit him. The visit seems so surreal at first because Prez hasn't had any connection to blood family since he was 5 years old.

When Jean saw Prez all emotions came rushing in because he hasn't seen him since he was a small child and he looked so much like his father. Jean hugged Prez so tight he didn't want to let him go.

He gave Khandi and Savius a big hug as well. He was already familiar with them since Prez talked about them in the letters he wrote to Jean and he had spoken to them on more than one occasion when he would call Prez.

"Damn Prezden, you the splitting image of your mother and father. Look at you, you a grown as man now."

"I know Cousin Jean, if it wasn't for the pictures that Aunt V left behind, everything would just continue to be faded memories."

"So Cousin Jean, I hired a lawyer to review your case. We working on getting you up out of here. His name is Richard Sabree, he a Muslim dude, real good with his work, tried some of the best cases. He'll be contacting you soon."

"Lil Cuzzo, I love you man. You won't regret anything. It's because of you, that now I don't look at things in this world the same as I did over a decade ago. After losing your pops, moms and my mom's and being up in here all these years I had just given up. But now I have you back in my life, and my new family." Turning to Khandi and Savius, "I see hope, I see change. Your parents would be so proud to see how you turned out. You young, doing your thing and you're responsible. Whatever you doing, you have order and with that you gonna always be on top."

"I've learned from some of the best. My adoptive parents taught me a lot, Major has been my front runner. He always told me you have to take care of yourself in order to help others and always keep your shit in order, cause once you do that your business will have order."

CHAPTER EIGHTEEN

One Saturday afternoon, Prezden and Khandi took a ride over to Brooklyn. He left Mateo in charge of things for the day. Prez wanted to look at the house he once lived in when he was only a young child. They get to the house and Prez got out the car and rang the bell.

An older gentleman by name of Mr. Gray had appeared at the door. Prez started conversation with the man and explained his history and connection to the property. At first Mr. Gray was a little apprehensive until he saw Khandi approaching. They stood on the doorstep and talked for a while. He even allowed Khandi and Prez to come inside and look around. It was a very emotional time for Prez. Prez stated that he was interested in buying the property. Mr. Gray was actually very open to the idea since his wife had passed away a few years back and his children lived out of state he basically felt he out grew the property and really had hopes of moving back down south a place he called home.

Prez also inquired about the vacant property right next door. Mr. Gray told him that the previous owners had lost it because they had defaulted on the taxes. He told Prez to contact the County courthouse to get more information about it. Prez and Mr. Gray exchanged numbers so that they can further discuss the possibility of him selling Prez and Khandi the house. Since they had already been talking about buying a house, they actually were considering buying the exact house he lived in as a child. They wanted to look into it a little further.

Two weeks later Prez and Khandi go to the County court house and got information on the house next door. They found out that it was up for a tax lien sale. Prez purchased that house shortly after. He and Mr. Gray worked out a deal that was suitable for both of them and Prez purchased that house as well. Prez contacted Darnell, Mr. Valentine's former business partner. He and Prez kept in contact occasionally over the years. Darnell kind of always felt that Prez would end up doing different things other than what his parents would approve of. He used to tell Mr. Valentine to keep a close eye on him being down at the projects. But at the end of the day, he decided to just let it go and let Prez live his life, but he was only a phone call away if he needed help or advice. They brainstormed over the architectural layout of how Prez and Khandi wanted their house to be.

Meanwhile business was booming, money was flowing in smoothly. Savius was feeling this life and going back to school was no longer a thought. Savius's mind frame had changed. He was making that fast money and lots of it he practically had to force Ms. Lexi out of the projects. He brought a two bedroom condo in Brooklyn, very close to where Prez would soon be living. They kept the apartment in the PJ's going for their own personal use.

Ms. Anne refused to let her apartment go, she was used to living in the projects, she knew the neighborhood well, had all her friends there and she wasn't having it. Khandi begged her to consider things after they were finished getting the house together. She eventually said that she would think about it. After things were finalized and she saw the outcome she undoubtedly changed her mind and moved in. She had her own separate area of the house and she loved it.

It took some time a lot of work and effort to get things the way they envisioned it to be. It took almost a year, but it was well worth the patience, hard work and time put into it. The house was complete from top to bottom and it was beautiful. When they were done the two houses became a double house. It remained a separate unit from the outside but on the inside they were adjoined by a huge sliding glass door on the first floor and double stair leading to the 2nd floor. Leaving full access to every room on both sides of the house.

Prez continued his relationship with Jean, and keeping him up to date of things happening in his life. He mailed pictures of the new house to Jean and he absolutely loved it. Mr. Sabree had contacted Jean and went over the details of the case. He was working diligently to get Jean released.

After fully furnishing and decorating the house, Prez and Khandi planned their house warming for July 8th. They sent out invitations to a chosen few. The very day of the house warming party Prez and Savius go to the Ralph Lauren store to purchase an outfit for the party tonight at Prez's house. The shopkeeper is helping a customer; she looks over at Prez and Savius.

"I'll be with you gentlemen in a moment. Take your time and feel free to look around."

Prez and Savius explore the store seeking out their interest. The shopkeeper walks over to them and introduces herself.

"Hi my name is Dana and I'll be assisting you. Is there anything in particular you two fine gentlemen are focused on purchasing today?"

Savius turns to Dana.

"Well I'm looking for something reserved to a certain extent."

"And what about yourself?" Glancing over at Prez.

"I'm on some official shit."

"What type of occasion is it?"

“Well my boy here brought a house and he’s breaking in the grounds tonight.”

“Congratulations, follow me think I may have something just right you, but it may take a while for you Mr. Reserved.”

Dana sashays across the room like she was in a beauty pageant or something. Savius eyes supervise her figure in the navy blue Ralph Lauren knitted dress she was wearing. She slides out a stepladder and sift through the clothing. She pulls out a dark gray Ralph Lauren Suit, reaches over and hands Prez a black dress shirt.

“What do you think of this?”

“Looking good, where’s the fitting room?”

“The fitting room is to the far left corner of the store, you can try that on while I help your friend.” She says with a slick smile on her face.

“Now, let me start by taking your measurements.”

“How come you didn’t ask to take my boys measurements?”

“I estimated him, but you? Hmm. (smiling) you’re not so easy to figure out.”

“And why is that?”

“I want to make sure that whatever I recommend for you is exact from head to toe.”

After she takes his measurements she walks over to the garment rack, tugs down a navy blue and cream Ralph Lauren sweater and a pair of navy blue slacks.

“I think blue should be your color.”

“The way you wearing that dress, It’s definitely yours.”

“Thank you, I hope your girl don’t mind you throwing out compliments like that.”

“I’ll have to find out when I get one. I hope your man don’t mind you accepting compliments like that, especially from a total stranger.”

"I'll have to find out when I get one and maybe you won't have to be a total stranger much longer, unless you choose to be."

"Well why don't we get acquainted by having you come to the party tonight?"

"I close shop at five call me."

She starts writing her number down, when Prez walks up and says, "Is this me or what Dog?"

"That's you, that's official my dude."

"Yes, that's perfect."

Dana hands Savius her number. Prez and Savius split and go their separate ways to get ready for tonight's affair. When Savius reached home, he passes time making an addition to his call list by programming Dana's number into his phone. Hours go by and he gives Dana a call.

He walks over to the white Formica end table and picks up the hands free cordless phone and begins to sound dial. Although, Dana practically petitioned his interest, she had already predetermined that if he actually called, she would estimate his curiosity by letting the phone ring at least four times before answering. She didn't want to give the impression that she was just raring to go. Savius was just about to dead the line when Dana picked up.

"Hello?" She answered with a false sense of composure in her voice. I mean you can tell she was just about ready to inflate from the thrill that he actually called. They begin conversation with the basic information flow.

"So Savius tell me about yourself?"

"What do you want to know?"

"As much to be expected from someone I'm just meeting today."

"Well, I'm not a knotty cat so; there isn't a lot to tell. I'm 21, have no kids, no special someone right now. I hold my own, no time for games, earning my ends and trying to live more than just comfortable."

"Alright, I'm definitely feeling you."

"So what you all about?"

"I'm about exploring the finer things in life, adventure and basically having fun. I have no kids, my own place, I love music especially jazz. I'm 24; I just celebrated my birthday last month. I'm originally from Boston. I kind of outgrew things over there so I moved to New York about two years ago to advance my career in fashion. Besides this is where the liveliness is anyway. Well enough about me I've been talking up a storm and you hardly said much."

"It's cool; I don't mind taking notes while you chew the fat. I'm not much of a telephone person anyway unless it's business or something brief. So if you find me damaged on words it's because this is not my natural channel of communication."

"Chew that fat, what does that mean"?

"It means chatter."

Savius replies with laughter in his voice.

"So your name is Savius, that's a nice name, it's different."

"Thank you, I'm grateful."

"What's your family name?"

"My last name is Lexington."

"I'm impressed."

"Impressed by what?"

"Well most of the time when I first meet a man, they seem to have a problem revealing their complete name. I feel as though they're holding back a big part of who they really are and eventually I'll end up with glitches, but you didn't waiver."

"I look at it like this, everybody has their own limitations and in this situation I didn't opt for my last name to be one of them. A person is as deep as they allow you to dig. I don't want to give the wrong impression that I'm totally unrestricted."

"So you're a business man huh? What kind of business are you into?"

"Import and export of urban distribution."

"Oh ok, and what do you do for pleasure?"

"Well it depends and speaking of pleasure what's up with tonight, you still rolling with me or what'?"

"Oh, no doubt. What time are you picking me up?"

"I got a few more things to finish up here, I can settle on 10:00."

Dana provides Savius with her address towards the closing of the conversation. Dana is keyed up in connection with partying tonight in the company of Savius. She swiftly makes her way to the bedroom and opens the closet door to see what she can exhume.

Surprisingly just about every article of clothing in her possession seemed too bargained or just put together and didn't tribute her enough to illustrate her true craft for style. Dana takes a quick look through the closet one last time, similar to an illegal search or something startling.

She makes her way to the rear of the closet and she comes across an indigo blue Cashmere Anne Klein dress that she paid a great deal of money for at a fashion show two years ago, when she first moved to New York. After stepping out of a hot peach fragranced bubble bath, Dana tried on the dress before establishing that this would be her final selection.

She took a look in the mirror and referred to the entire fit as faultless. Dana deposits a few finishing touches to her now controlled hairdo. She pours herself a glass of white wine and waits for Savius to arrive. She suddenly remembered that the little sticky tag with her apartment number had fallen off the panel next to the intercom. She decided to meet Savius downstairs because she wasn't sure if he would know which bell to ring since he never asked her last name and her first name was initialed.

She steals a look at the clock and its 9:58 PM. She sprinkles on a delicate scent, snatches her coat and keys along with her purse and begins walking briskly toward the front door. The doorbell rings, she glances down at her wristwatch and it's 10:00 on the dot. She presses the talk button.

"Who is it?"

"It's Savius."

"I'll be right down."

She says with an undisturbed manner in her voice. She enters the elevator, smoothing on some lipstick while providing herself with a last minute appraisal through the mirrors on the elevator doors.

Savius positioned himself on the set of stairs in front of the building facing the doorway. Dana walks out and they both investigate one another without delay.

"What's up Ms. Porter? Damn don't you look red carpet!"

"Thank you and it's explicit that you provide true flavor to that outfit. There's definitely no comparison to displaying it in the store and what I'm catching sight of right now."

"Thanks, and you're more than welcome. You know I can appreciate a woman who can take delivery of a compliment and give one out also."

"Well I can respect a man willing to donate one in specially selected taste."

Savius escorts Dana across the street to his emerald green Q45. They get in and navigate their way to the party. With steady conversation flowing and gentle music playing in the background Dana sensed she was in good company.

"You know I went to school for a minute in Boston?"

"Really? What school did you attend?"

"Boston College in Chestnut Hill."

"Oh, Wow! Okay I went to Boston College High School." She gives a pleasant smile.

"Strange little coincidence huh?" Savius says while looking over at Dana.

"Yes it is. So Savius what year did you graduate?"

"I didn't. Long story short, I went up on a basketball scholarship, had a bad fall. Dislocated my shoulder and tore my ACL and I ended up back home."

"Sorry to hear that."

"Thanks but I'm good. It was a good experience and I don't regret anything. I love to ball and I hoped that would be my ticket out the hood at the time. But God is good because business is good, life is good and I wouldn't have it any other way."

"That's great, not a lot of people can say the same."

"Yeah."

They pull up in front of the house and walk in together. Dana felt uncomfortable by the way certain individuals were staring at her. She felt like she was performing in concert in front of a live audience or something.

Since Dana wasn't familiar with anyone else there, she kept close to Savius to validate that she was his guest. At first she was intimidated by the large amount of people constantly acknowledging Savius presence. He was obviously a well-known and liked person, but the way he stayed in control and by no means changed his persona helped to make her feel secure the remainder of the evening.

They advanced their way thru the house headed towards Prez and Khandi. Savius introduced Dana to Khandi and to Prez once again. Khandi and Prez both welcomed Dana to their new home.

"Congratulations to both of you on your very attractive home."

Prez and Khandi express their thanks.

"Yo Save man I need to subtract you for a minute. I got shit I want to discuss with you right quick. Khandi why don't you show Dana around? You cool with that Dana? My baby will take care of you."

"Hey, no snags here."

"Yeah we get to talk about you for a little while Save." Khandi says in a jokingly way.

"Nah, I'm joking this is my boy right here. Come on Dana let me show you the rest of the house."

"Yo Save man you were grave and shit about hooking up with honey huh?"

"Yeah dog, she gave me a bit of a zing at the store, so you know maybe we can swing an episode or two."

"You know Khandi gonna crash her mind to see if she's decent enough for you."

"Oh for sure, but its all love. I know Khandi's gonna keep it real looking out for me or whatever. But y'all know me. I'm just chillin from this point on I aint goin underground with nobody right now ya heard? Anyway, where's swift and the rest of them grimy dogs?"

"They downstairs shooting pool and losing all their doe to Major. Let's go thrash em just for the hell of it." Savius and Prez go downstairs to join in a game of pool.

Dana accompanies Khandi into the complete black and ivory kitchen and they make their way across the glossy marble flooring. Dana observes the stone top Island in the center of the floor and the unique set of cast iron pots draping from the swivel rack. Dana touches the pots sending them in a swinging motion.

"I really like this, was it difficult mounting?"

"Prez and Savius installed it and they said it was pretty simple. Trust me if those two are accountable for this, then it wasn't difficult at all."

"It appears to be very durable. To be frank I always said that one day when I buy a house I would have one of these in my kitchen. It puts me in mind of the old black and white Negro classics that I used to watch years ago and it always caught my attention. I haven't seen cast iron pots and pans in years. They don't make them like this anymore. I know this must have been pretty costly."

"Yeah well we paid a silver dollar but sometimes you have to spend the extra ends for hand -picked value. I know that you have a handle on what I'm saying. As plain as the nose on my face you didn't short change on that Anne Klein dress you're sporting."

"You have a sharp eye. I didn't think anyone would identify what designer I was wearing, especially since I brought this at a fashion show two years ago."

"I have a dress similar to that, except it's white, sleeveless and just a little bit shorter. I love Anne K's clothing. I can recognize her work in a minute."

"Girl you have to show me the dress you talking about. It seems we have related taste."

"Yeah, so far we speak the same language. So Dana how long have you known Save?"

"Well believe it or not, we just met earlier today. He and Prez both came into the shop where I work looking for something to wear tonight. We started talking or whatever, exchanged numbers and tada! Here I am. I don't normally do stuff like this but he just seems so cool and down to earth on top of being so damn fine. Not to mention, the one whiff of that Issey Miake cologne he was wearing he had my undivided attention."

"I hear you. Well you're right about him being cool and down to earth. I've known Save practically all my life and we're pretty tight. He's like a brother to me you know? So you work at the Ralph Lauren store downtown? Do you live in that area?"

"Yeah, I've been living downtown for about two years now. I moved here from Boston."

"Oh, did Save tell you he went to school in Boston?"

"Yeah he mentioned it."

"So what brings you to the big apple?"

"There was a combination of things. I mean I occupied 22 years of my life there and it was time for a change. Like I was telling Savius, I basically outgrew things over there. Plus my key goal was to follow my fascination for fashion."

"Oh that's cool. Listen, can I get you something to eat or drink?"

"No thanks, I'm good right now. But I would love the chance to see the rest of the house. I'm so excited. This is my first time ever seeing a double house."

"You know, Prez used to live in this house when he was a kid. There's a lot of history here. To make a long story short he wanted to buy this and the one next door just so happen to be up for sale so he came up with the idea of buying both and joining them. I must say that he is quite a creative man."

"Wow! Ok that would be an understatement." Dana says while looking around with an inquisitive look on her face.

"Okay, let me show you the dining room."

Khandi and Dana continue to chat. They enter the dining room and the first thing Dana notices is the huge cherry oak double pedestal table which seats ten.

"Put my name down for reservations, I want to be here for the Thanksgiving feast."

Taking a deep breath, Dana pulls back a chair and takes a seat. She gazes up at the sparkling crystal diamond shaped chandelier, and in her mind she just increased the value of the room.

"Khandi I'll have a glass of white wine. That's if you have?"

"Sure, I have a Vouvray, white burgundy and Sancerre. Which would you prefer?"

"I haven't had a white burgundy in a while, so I'll take that."

"Khandi I see you know a thing or two about your wines."

"A little something. I crutch off of Prez, when his parents were alive they were collectors. So we have a big selection down in the cellar."

"Be right back, make yourself comfortable."

While Khandi goes to the cellar, that she calls her little underground store at times, Dana seizes the moment to finish admiring the setup of the enormous room. She walks over to the china cabinet. Checking out the mirror back halogen lit interior thru the beveled glass doors. Her curiosity brings her over to the window. She is anxious to sneak a quick peek at the backyard. She pulls back the crimson velvet drapes and catches a full view.

The backyard was so huge that it fit four patio sets, a flower garden and vegetable garden that was openly in progress, a miniature basketball court, a tool shed and a large tree of some sort. Dana's attention was so absorbed into gazing at the backyard that she failed to notice when Khandi had re-entered the room. Holding two wine glasses in her hands Khandi says, "Let's just say, that section of the house is still in the works."

Dana was caught in a moment of awkwardness at the time because she had planned on returning back to her seat before Khandi would come back. She didn't want it to look like she was doing her own little research. To Dana this would only make her seem as if she had lost her composure. In other words seem overwhelmed with her surroundings. So in order to break the uneasiness she was feeling at the time, she turns to Khandi and says, “Nice patio set. That’s made by Chelsea right?”

“Thanks, girl I can’t begin to tell you, it was a gift from a family friend. I don’t mean to sound unappreciative, but I actually had a bamboo set in mind. But we’ll definitely make the most of it for sure. So here’s your wine, let’s toast to new beginnings.”

They both clang their glasses together and take a sip of their drinks.

“Delicious.”

“I’ll finish showing you around, and then we can go downstairs with the guys. Save must have asked for you about three times within the ten minutes I was down there. He must be digging you girl.”

Dana looks up with a self-controlled smile on her face. She really wanted to blush hard, but instead she chose to lift the glass to her lips and sip the wine as gracefully as possible. They finish drinking their wine and venture off to the living room. As they entered the living room, Dana felt like she had just walked into leather land.

After being hit with the unmistakable scent of brand new leather and running her hand across the honey maple supple soft leather three piece sectional, leather ottoman and leather top multi-tier cocktail table.

She thought to herself. “Damn there’s enough leather in this room to tailor my very own coat, handbag shoes and then some.”

Dana simply sized up the room and emphasized on how enormous it was, as if it was the finest quality of the whole entire unit. The way she carried on you would think she was talking about legroom inside of a car or something. She didn’t want to make a fuss over the luxuriousness so she tried to touch on space and foundation as if this really attached as a rule to be the most important thing to her.

While Dana was babbling on, Khandi's best friend Donna was passing by and she whispered to Khandi.

"Damn why don't she just knock down the building and draw up a new blue print."

They both laughed out loud. Khandi didn't want Dana to realize the joke was about her, so she quickly introduced both girls in a friendly manner. Khandi was a little on edge because she knows Donna can be hypersensitive and a little ahead of her time. Especially when she's had a little Bacardi or Vodka in her system.

Khandi can just feel the negative behavior about to expand just by the way Donna was looking Dana up and down. She told Donna that she would meet her downstairs, in a short while after she was finished showing Dana the house.

"You need to be showing her ass the door." Donna said as she walked out of the room.

"Dana, I apologize, she just had a little too much to drink. She doesn't really mean any harm."

"Look I'm here on social terms, not for combat. Besides I might of heard a bit or piece of what was being said by why even bother to give the feedback she was obviously looking for? This is just typical behavior when you knock back more than one glass of something as a thirst quencher, instead of sipping and tasting as a stimulant. I guess for some that's the liquid remedy to their problems. Oh, well some people just can't control their liquor."

"I understand you may have caught offense, but like I said she meant no harm."

Although, Donna was obviously in the wrong she was still Khandi's best friend, so she started to take offense. She had to hurry and change the subject before the tongue lashing got any deeper.

"Would you like to go Join Save now, or finish looking around?"

"I'm good, let's finish the tour."

Khandi decided to show her the library next. Dana shadowed Khandi so close that she darkened her every footstep. As they entered the library, Dana's attention is directed toward the faint light beaming down from the ceiling. She notices the large skylight, covering a huge portion of the ceiling. Since it was night time she was able to capture the perfect view of the midnight blue sky and the star light glow. Khandi walks over to the console table and flicks on the lamp.

"Wow! Imagine that during the daylight hours any extra lighting in here would be unnecessary."

"Except for when I'm reading or writing, I feel the need to use as much light as possible."

"What's this?"

Picking up a book that was lying on the end of one of the tables.

"Oh that's a book I'm reading called, *Flipped*. It's really interesting. The main character kind of puts me in the mind of Prez."

"Is it good so far?"

"It's definitely a page turner, when I'm done you can read it if you like."

"Okay, Cool."

"Is that a massage chair"?

"Yes girl. I come in here just to relax and think sometimes you know, to clear my mind and chill. It has a built in sound system that plays all kinds of peaceful tunes of nature while melting away any type of stress. I usually end falling asleep in here. Especially, on rainy days."

"Oh I know exactly what you talking about. I sleep like a baby on rainy days."

Dana walks over to the double arch bookcase admiring all the books on the shelves. They had everything from encyclopedias, dictionaries', paperbacks, hardbacks, cookbooks, newspapers, glossy magazines etc...

Dana notices a set of 2 copper trunks and she is curious to know what's inside.

"Oh is this where you keep all your hidden treasures?"

"You are absolutely right."

Khandi walks over to the antique looking trunks an opens one up. She pulls out a scrap book.

"These are pictures from back in the days from Junior high school and high school."

"Oh, I see you were a cheerleader. Wait a minute is that Savius?"

She zooms in on the picture of Savius wearing his basketball uniform.

"Yes, that's ya boy Save, and that's Prez right there."

"Number 24 huh? That just so happens to be my favorite number. It's the day I was born. June 24th."

They continued to scan through different pages of the scrapbook, graduation books, and different photo albums as they laughed and talked.

"What's inside this trunk?"

"Oh, that's nothing."

"Oh, is it empty?"

"No, it's not empty, but you wouldn't want to see that stuff."

"Come on Khandi, why not?" Dana says with a sneaky little smile covering her face.

"That stuff is so prehistoric and in poor condition, let's keep it moving."

"Oh Khandi, I find that hard to believe, with all the backdated stuff you just put on view and it's all in mint condition. I think you're trying to pull my leg come on let's see."

"Dana, you are a persistent little something huh? True to life it's personal. My parents wedding album, pictures of my mom when she was still alive, Pictures of Prez's deceased Parents, both sets at that."

"Both sets?" She bypasses Dana's question.

"You see, these things are very sentimental and I'd rather not open Pandora's Box."

Dana is standing there thinking of a way to pull her foot out of her mouth. She certainly didn't want to rub Khandi the wrong way. So changing the subject, she asked if she could take a look through the solid brass telescope mounted on the tripod near the window. She takes a look, pulling it upward, facing the skylight, zooming in on the stars and crystal clear view of the moon.

"This is really beautiful. If this was a few days ago, I would have been able to capture that full moon we had. Well maybe next time."

Khandi had kind of had enough alone time with Dana. Especially after she was being super nosey about the contents in the trunk. But Khandi held her composure, turning her down as gracefully as she possible could imagine. Thank goodness Donna wasn't around at the time. They join the other guest. Dana is back in the company of Savius. And they partied the rest of the night away.

CHAPTER NINETEEN

Dana and Savius continue their association and its development over the next few weeks. They spent a lot of time with Prez and Khandi. They would dine at fancy restaurants, go to the movies, they caught a few Broadway shows and they would chill out at Prez and Khandi's house.

When Prez and Savius were occupied with business, Dana would make it her business to get up with Khandi and they would go to fashion shows, they would go shopping together buying expensive clothing, shoes and jewelry. The two went to an art show one time and Dana purchased a very pricey painting for $2,000.00 dollars. Dana knew she was living above and beyond her means, maxing out her credit cards and reducing her bank account, but she was determined to keep up with the sort of lifestyle that came natural to Khandi.

No matter what Khandi was used to having nice things from day one, but if you let Dana tell it, this is what she was used to as well. Dana made it known that back in Boston her family was pretty well off. She said her father was a Doctor and her mother was a Seamstress and this is what really sparked her interest for fashion.

Donna wasn't comfortable with all the mixing and mingling between the two. She didn't trust Dana and in her opinion she felt Dana was just kissing Khandi's ass, as a way of sealing approval intended for Savius. In other words she was using Khandi as her little hallmark. Also, since Donna and Khandi were best friends, she felt that Dana was carving up the time they would normally spend together.

In reality there was always an open invitation for Donna and her boyfriend Chuck to hang out with the group and do the couple's thing, but it wouldn't happen because he wasn't around as much. He landed a job working as a computer software programmer. He worked long hours and he traveled a lot. This left Donna feeling left out. But when they were not doing the couples thing and Khandi was solo, she would call Donna, but the plans seemed to include Dana on the regular and Donna was not feeling that at all.

One day Khandi called Donna and asked her to take a ride with her over to Dana's house to pick up a diamond tennis bracelet she let Dana borrow. Donna immediately started going off.

"Khandi I can't believe you let that toffee –nosed wannabe borrow your shit. Are you crazy? Besides if she supposed to be full of this and that why couldn't she go out and buy her own shit? Why she gotta be perpetrating frauds in yours like she really about something!"

"Look Donna, I'm in the middle of the road when it comes to you two. She seems to be on the up and up to me and besides you know she keeping a smile on Saves face so I'm cool."

"On the up and up huh? I don't really think so. Maybe to the casual observer but out of the ordinary she seems to have yawl asses fooled."

"Do I detect a little jealousy?"

"Yeah, girl you do from her to you. I mean just take the time out to see just how she tries to mimic you."

"Why would she need to do that? She has a mind of her own and she's her own person."

"Oh, really? So why is she always trying to keep up with you and copy your style. She trying hard to become a mini you and each time you fuck with her, you making it real easy for her to do just that."

"Donna you're tripping right now. That girl is a grown ass woman who is obviously holding her own and it appears that she is about something."

"Awl isn't that cute. Listen to you and how you fluffing her wig. I don't care what you say; she's giving a false impression about something."

"Listen Donna, it looks like she's gonna be around for a minute so why don't you at least try to get to know her better. The last thing I want to do is bring unnecessary drama to Save. So how about it? Besides I miss my best friend we haven't chilled together since yesteryear."

"You know what Khandi girl, you're right. Okay, I'll do it for you. What time you coming to get me?"

"Love you bad girl .Smooches! I'll be there in an hour."

Khandi stops by Donna's house to pick her up and they head over to Dana's. When they arrive at Dana's, Khandi rings the intercom and announces that she is downstairs. Dana has a very pleasant and bubbly tone in her reply and she buzzes them in. When they get upstairs to the apartment and Dana opens the front door she has a disappointed look on her face when she sees Donna.

Dana cracks a phony smile. She speaks and invites them inside the apartment. Donna caught on to the bullshit right away, so she decided to be just as shitty in spite of the conversation that she and Khandi had earlier.

"Oh Dana, this is a cute little cubicle you have here."

Donna peaks around the wall looking at the small bedroom. "And Oh I like the way they put up this little dividing wall and the cute little space just enough for you to fit that twin size bed and ooh that adorable miniature dresser. I know you must be glad that you live alone cause imagine more than one person trying to bunk on that, someone would surely fall off and bump their head. Wow a twin size; I haven't seen one of those since I was a kid."

"Well actually this is what you call a studio apartment, in case you really don't know. And as for the twin size bed, it's no problem for someone like me with a cute petite little figure. And with the right size individual it's a perfect size."

Khandi quickly interrupts by asking Dana for a glass of water. Dana walks off to the kitchen to get the water for Khandi.

"Donna, come on what did we just talk about? I thought you was gonna be better than this?"

"I was but she started this whole thing from the moment she open the door and shot me look daggers."

"That's my fault, I tried to call her to let her know I was bringing company, but her line was busy the whole time."

"Company? Oh, I'm company now?"

"You know what I mean. So stop acting like a child and just be nice."

Dana enters the room and hands Khandi the glass of water. She goes into the bedroom and comes back with the bracelet Khandi came by to pick up.

"Khandi, thanks again you're a lifesaver girl."

"Yeah, that was very sweet of Khandi to let you hold that. She always has been the type to help the needy."

"Well obviously she didn't help you dress yourself today. You should have done at least one more dress rehearsal before leaving the house in the mix and match you threw together."

Dana walks away after the quick tongue lashing she just threw out to Donna.

"You must have put a lot of practice into that stank ass walk of yours."

"Some things just come natural to a real lady."

"What does being a real lady have to do with your equilibrium being off?"

"What?"

"Ladies! Ladies! Come on now. You've both said more than enough. When is this all going to stop? Like I told you earlier Donna, this is so childish and it's only right that I tell you the same Dana. Come on we're all adults here. So let's act like it. Listen Dana I'm gonna leave now and I'll talk with you later. Donna come on let's go." Donna walks away with a ready look on her face.

CHAPTER TWENTY

Several months pass by; in spite of the bad mouthing Dana received from Donna, she and Savius lengthen their involvement. They began getting together on a more individual setting. Dana felt that a steady relationship was on the rise.

Savius kept both feet on the ground and made it no secret that he wasn't ready for a bigger picture. Dana was willing to take on the challenge of becoming Savius's woman in her mind. She was the materialistic type and she was drawn to Savius because he had lots of money, drove a swanky whip, dressed really nice, was popular, powerful and extremely attractive. What more could she possibly ask for.

She referred to him as the perfect man. She was determined that things would become more intense over time, the status would change and she would surely hook the man she so badly desired. She wanted to fit in and do things the traditional way and be accepted. Dana tried for a long time to brush her true feelings under the carpet but her emotions became highly sensitive in the long run. See things began to change and the time they would spend together slowly began to fall off.

At the start of the relationship phase they pushed off with partying together, socializing with different acquaintances and close friends, going to a variety of places and playing house. Their mingling seemed like the perfect blend. That was up until Pez and Savius started facing off about the time Savius was spending away from the business.

"What's up Mr. Happy?"

"What's up?"

Savius lays his hand on his chest, and looks at Prez with a raised eyebrow.

"What's with the Mr. Happy stuff?"

"Cause right now, I would say you real happy go lucky, and that's cool but you not taking care of business Save man and that's the part that aint cool."

"How long can I run business on a skeleton crew? You know Raze is out of town for a minute, Roof is handling business with his Moms being ill right now, Swift and Mateo taking turns standing in for you doing their job and yours and that shit aint good by me."

"So you saying I'm changing direction? That I'm sitting on my heels?"

"Well yeah, you just said it, so yeah fuck yeah. I thought you and Dana was on some fun time, but nah this is real time. Dana done watered you down man, it's time to float up, come on we the rock of this shit and I can't keep being your talking head when you not on the job Save. You gotta get your mind right yo, you too cozy."

"So you saying I can't have a personal life? Do I fucks with you when you and Khandi are chillin do y'all own thang?"

"Yo! Khandi been around from the beginning of time and shit. She knows and understands the business and the difference between me and you right now is that my shit is like clockwork all the time. You be postponing shit, busting up in the eleventh hour and it's causing problems. You becoming too motherfucking disorderly. Like I said get ya mind right!"

You can tell Savius was starting to feel some kind of way about what Prez was saying to him. His whole body language and facial expressions changed. But he stood there and kept his mouth closed and let Prez go ahead and say whatever it was he needed to say to him.

"I can't afford to be easy on your ear right now Save, I have to call it how I know it is. Come on, niggas talking about you running your term and making a come up on your spot, due to your lack of and I can't let that happen. You my right hand, we the rock."

"I stood here and listened to everything you said. I don't even have a comeback. You right and I'm willing to carry the can, you talkin real talk. I'm about to make a U-turn and get back in order."

Savius had a lot of love and respect for Prez. One face off was all it took for him to get back on track and keep his priorities in order. They got passed Savius issues and continued to talk.

"Prez, by the way, I know you were trying to be general when you said niggas was talkin. But I know it was that wannabe motherfucker Mateo. I aint been feeling him for a while. I think we ought a drop that nigga. I been heard he been running his mouth lately."

"Running his mouth about what?"

"He's been talking big shit about you. How you wasn't supposed to be the one on the next, it should have been him. You was a Cosby kid so you got doe already. You know just talking smack cause he secretly hating."

"Cosby Kid huh! Ha! That's some funny fucking shit. I'm a put a closer eye on that dude."

"Yo Prez, chill why you making that face? You got the crazy wrinkle nose going on right now." Savius asked Prez while laughing.

"Cause I'm smelling fish right now."

"We gonna check that shit ASAP, one way or another. Now check out my wrinkle nose, when I say. Chill on the Mr. Happy shit alright, I'm just chillin with Dana and having fun."

"Aww come on now, you already know I'm coming with the jokes, but for real it aint like I said there was something wrong with being happy though. So what's up with you and Dana, you trying to make it happen or what? Cause I think you feelin her more than you care to say."

"Nah dog! She a good girl and everything but I like I said before and keep saying, I'm just having fun. I aint making anybody a title holder any time soon. Off that, what's been good? Do I have to run down and re-introduce myself to niggas again?"

"Nah you good, just get up and stay up."

"That's what's good. So what's up with Jean, he getting ready get out soon?"

"Yeah things are looking real good for him. I think he'll be out soon, like a year or so, hopefully sooner. But on the real, he's been locked down for 16 years so another year or so aint gonna set him back."

"Yeah that's true. He a real cool dude, I can't wait for him to get out though. You my brother from another Mother, so that's Big Cuz, addition to the family you heard?"

"No doubt."

They double up, talk over business and come to solid agreements. For Savius it was an uphill struggle finding middle ground between dedicating time to the business and knocking together enough time to spend with Dana.

CHAPTER TWENTY-ONE

A month rolls by and Savius is back on track with business. Whenever he and Prez would discuss business details, they would meet at the car wash and they would refer to it as the wetlands. They figured this was one of the safest places to talk because you never know whose listening.

One day Savius was in the warehouse counting money and supplies and things just wasn't adding up correctly. He wanted to get on top of the problem right away and bring it to Prez's attention. So he gave him a call.

"Yo Prez, meet me at the Wetlands in 45."

"Alright, but what's up? You sound like something wrong."

"We might have a problem, but just meet me and we'll get to it."

"Alright, One."

They end the quick conversation and Savius headed over to their meeting place. They would always drive separate vehicles and go thru the carwash in each vehicle so they can discuss whatever they need to discuss.

"So what's going on?"

"I was counting up money and product but shit aint adding up correctly. I think Mateo is up to some foul type shit. He's been balling out a lot lately. I got a feeling shit been going on for a while. Nigga got a new ride and popping those bottles hard up in the club and making it rain from what I hear. I know you make it possible for him to eat, but this nigga been feasting."

"Word?"

Prez has a very serious straight look on his face. He had no look of anger, no look of surprise it was basically expressionless and hard to read.

"I know Roof and Raze aint on no shit like that and the lil homies don't even have that kind of access, so I know it's that nigga Prez. And all that shit he running with lately, that nigga crooked Prez."

"Ok, we can get a crooked nigga straight. Let's run him back on day one. Put that nigga on dummy run."

What Prez is referring to, is the test runs he learned Major had put him and Savius through when they first started running with him.

Instead of supplying them with real goods and products, it would really be fakes. This way if the fake stuff went into circulation and it ever came back to be a problem, he would know exactly who the culprit was.

Prez and Save discussed to what degree they would go about doing this. Prez contacted one of his connects named Chauncey and he explained that there was gonna be a drop off, but the shit was gonna be a dud because he was testing a nigga out. Chauncey agreed and they put the plan in motion. Prez sent Mateo on a drop off to Chauncey and they just chilled and waited for the outcome.

Later that night, Prez, Savius, Roof, Swift and Raze was at the warehouse counting money and doing a re-up when all of a sudden there was a loud banging at the door. Swift went to the door, with his 9 ready for whatever.

"Yo who dat?"

"It's Curly."

"Fuck you want nigga?"

"I need to holler at Prez."

"Fuck you want nigga?"

Curly top is this puffed up goon, who bounces down at one of the strip joints in the cut on the west side called Najee's. He gets high off coke and smoke a little weed from time to time. He's been a long standing customer ever since Major was running shit around the way. Prez never conducts business at the warehouse and niggas haven't seen him in a while, so they knew right away something was up. Swift turns to Prez for the verdict and he gave Swift the go ahead to let him in.

"Nah go ahead let him in yo."

Swift slowly opens the door, Curly top is standing there with this wild look in his eyes, face and hair covered in sweat, just looking sick.

"Yo Prez man what the fuck is this?"

Reaching in his pocket to pull something out, Swift draws on him.

"Whoa partner! Slow that shit down."

"Nah Swift leave it alone, he good let him finish doing what he do."

Curly top pulls out a baggie with a white substance in it and throws it on the floor. Roof runs up on him with his fist balled tight in the air yelling out.

"What the fuck nigga, you stupid or what? Pick that fucking shit up!"

"This shit is bogus, what do you want me to do?"

Prez intervenes because he knew off the top what this shit was about.

"Yo Curly man, you aint coming up in this piece on some rah rah. That's not how we doing shit around here. Pick the shit up and bring it over here."

Curly top bends down and picks the baggie up off the floor. Swift pats him down and he walks over to Prez handing him the baggie.

Prez opens the baggie and sticks his finger in the substance and just as he suspected it's baking soda instead of cocaine.

"Where you get this shit from my man?"

"I got it from your boy Mateo."

Savius turns to Prez.

"I told you that nigga was up to no fucking good."

Roof and the rest of them are in an uproar. There was so much being said at one time, the anger, the yells, the cursing and the threats are bouncing off the walls so loud that it sound like a growling pack of wolves was in the house.

Prez gave Curly top the real stuff in place of the bogus bull crap sold to him by Mateo. Prez told Curly top just take it and go do what he do don't fuck with Mateo and dead it once he walks out the door. As Curly top was walking out the door Prez called out to him to say one last thing.

"Yo Curly, you seen better days, I wanna see you with many more to come. Do me this, you gotta a problem, you got my number, you know any other way to find me rather than coming here and especially this time of night. So to avoid any conflict let's choose the easier route. I'm gonna say this one more time to make sure we clear. Keep it low; don't say shit to that nigga, bottom line I aint got time to be hunting for a nigga ya heard? Here take an extra bag, on me. Do you."

"I understand, we good it won't happen again."

Curly gets to the door, he looks over his shoulder at Roof. He felt nervous because everybody knows that dude is real quick with his hands. But Roof let him walk out without laying hands on him but his demeanor made it clear not to violate.

Prez and Savius closed shop and went home. Prez wanted to go home and sleep on how he was gonna handle things with Mateo. The next morning he called Savius and they met at the wetlands on 145th.

"Whadup?"

"Whadup?"

"Meet me at the wetlands in an hour."

"Alright One."

They get to the carwash and begin to talk.

"Yo Prez we aint gotta do a whole lot of talking about this shit. I can take care of that nigga myself. Show him what a pretty boy can do."

"Nah Save chill you good. Major coming down we gonna have a lil talk with that nigga."

"Aint nothing to talk about Prez, you too damn calm yo. If you was any calmer you'd be dead."

"That's how I'm supposed to be. He did what he did, so yeah there's a repercussion to his actions and he will get dealt with. Just keep shit in order, keep them niggas in order and I'll handle the rest."

CHAPTER TWENTY-TWO

Major made it around the way mid-afternoon. He and Prez ran Major's car through the car wash on 125 and Prez gave him the rundown on what happened. Major is very disappointed and upset. He feels bad because he was the one who suggested Prez keep Mateo on and working and he let him down.

"Yo Prez, I'm so fucking tight, I can kill that nigga with my bare hands right now. Matter fact I am gonna kill that nigga with my bare hands yo."

"Major, I got this, he been eating long enough, when I'm finish with him yo, he aint gonna wanna know shit else about this game. All the slick shit he been spittin behind a nigga back I aint call him on. Now he wanna take and steal from me?"

"Prez go ahead, call that nigga down here."

Prez called Mateo and told him to meet him down at the warehouse. Mateo had no clue that anything was wrong or that shit was about to go down, so he happily agreed and made his way to meet up with Prez. He does the special little knock that they do and Major opens the door and let him in.

"Eh Major what's up man?"

Mateo says with a flabbergasted tone in his voice. Major just gives him a head nod and pours a glass of scotch. Prez turns on the CD player. He pulls DMX "Flesh of My Flesh Blood of My Blood" CD from his case. He kept track 4: **Aint No Way** on repeat for the longest.

He presses play. Mateo is feeling that something is wrong because Major and Prez start talking over the music and acting like Mateo wasn't in their presence at first. He just stood there in deep thought trying to look unbothered. Major lights a cigar and passes one to Prez.

"So tell me lil bro, what would you say is the blueprint to your fortune?"

"Well big Bro, learning how to make sound decisions."

"And how do you go about doing that?"

"Trusting my judgment."

Prez turns to Major, "And how did you learn to trust your judgment?"

"By making not so sound decisions."

Prez faces Mateo, hands him a glass of Scotch. Mateo took the glass of scotch and threw it back in one shot; his nerves were a bit on edge.

"Mateo my nigga let me ask you this, would you rather cross a bridge or burn it?"

Mateo anxiously glimpsed back and forth at Prez, then Major and back at Prez again before answering the question.

"What?"

"Would you rather cross a bridge or burn one my Nigga? Wait before you answer that. Major what's your take on that?"

"Cross that mother fucker get to the other side, look back and know I accomplished something of course."

"Ok, so now my Nigga, Ima hit u with it again. What would you rather do? Cross a bridge or burn it?"

With a look of desperation he chuckles and gives a nervous shrug before answering.

"I don't know. Cross it I guess."

"So my Nigga, what happens if a bridge is burned?"

"I don't know, I guess you can't go back across that mother fucker. But what are you getting at?"

"Exactly, you can't go back across that mother fucker. Same goes for biting the hand that feeds you. You bite the hand that feeds you, you bite it off and it's gone. Now no more feeding, no more eating right? Now everybody fucked. Like X said bad decisions lead to last decisions. I believe the decisions you make can determine who you are. Not a bad analogy from the Cosby Kid huh?"

Mateo looks over at Major; you can tell he was expecting Major to step in and save him or something. He couldn't even look Prez in the face.

"Prez, you know you can't believe everything you hear."

He says while rubbing his hands and sweaty palms together.

"What you think I heard? Cause I aint get to it yet. So ok, since you think I heard something, fuck it. Do you have anything you wanna tell me?

Mateo drops his head, turning away from Prez.

"My nigga, real niggas give eye. I'm talking to you and you can stop gazing over at big bro. This is between me and you my nigga."

"Big bro me and this nigga, alright we need some me and him time. I'll hit you when I'm done."

Major looks at Mateo and he starts shaking his head.

"None of these other niggas out here had love for you. Just know that all your debts have to be paid. A bad, stupid choice is what you made. Prez Ima go holla at Mr. D. Hit me if you need me."

Major leaves Prez to handle his business with Mateo.

"My nigga, I provided you with more than enough steady work to keep your belly full right?"

"You right."

"So why you gotta get greedy on a nigga?"

"I don't know what you talking about. I holds it down and you know that Prez."

"Peeling off my mother fucking stash, tells me different. It tells me that you are a thief. That drop you made to Chauncey that was some bogus shit and you aint even know it. You turned around peeled off that and decided to do your own lil distribution. You hit that nigga Curly top and that shit came back to me. Nothing but pure baking soda, baking soda that I sent your fucking ass with. You aint waste no fucking time either."

Prez picks up the baggie that Curly top brought back to him and he threw it at Mateo.

"Taste that shit, you tell me what the fuck this is?"

"Taste like baking soda Prez."

"Exactly! Niggas tryna get high and you prepping niggas to bake mother fucking cakes?"

Mateo responds with a whiney low pitch in his voice.

'Yo Prez, this aint me, that's some bullshit. I would never do no shit like that. Come on man, check them other niggaz cause it wasn't me."

Prez gets real upset because Mateo continued to lie and not only that he started pointing the fingers at others. Prez starts to bark on him while clenching his hands together. He is really starting to lose patience with Mateo.

"You the only nigga I sent out with that shit, nigga don't fuck with me right now yo! It wasn't you huh? You want that to be your famous last words?"

Mateo felt uneasy and was not willing to admit his wrong doing. Instead the heat got turned up between the two.

"Nigga, this supposed to be my shit anyway. You aint Major and if anything you stole from me. You stole my fucking spot, brown nosing Major. You aint from these streets. You don't have that same thirst, you never did. You came down here from day one a lucky star. Fuck you want from down here? Who the one that's greedy? I been grinding down here, this is my way of life."

Mateo kept his eye on the 9 millimeter that was sitting on the table the whole time. He felt threatened that this meeting was not gonna end up well. He made a quick dash and grabbed up the gun. He looked up at Prez with unwavering eyes and drew the gun on Prez.

"Oh you gonna shoot me nigga, go ahead. Go head nigga, pull the trigger. You done turned it up now, no turning back."

Mateo stood there and without further thought he squeezed the trigger, Bop! And nothing happened. Prez is still standing there, not even a single hair on his head was disturbed.

He squeezed again, and for a second time. Bop! Yet again, nothing happened. Major and Mr. D came running downstairs quick fast. The scene was obvious and right off the top Major knew what went down. He turns to Mr. D.

"We got this Mr. D, you can go back up, we got this don't worry."

A minute later Save came bursting through the door.

"Fuck happened?"

"I'll tell you exactly what happened Save. This bitch ass, ungrateful, disloyal, worthless, dirtbag so called killer tried to murk me. Thought he had me on the slip. Nigga ran up with the prop gun my nigga and squeezed on me twice."

"Ahh yo ass dead now." Savius pulled out at 45 and was about to pop him. Major grabbed him.

"Yo Save let Prez decide what he wanna do with him and whatever it's gonna be, will be compliments of Prez."

Mateo tried copping a plea. He knew he fucked up big time and that death or something very close to it was upon him.

"Come on nigga, you gonna kill me? Listen I'm going thru a lot of shit right now."

Prez quickly cuts him off. "I could get you ready for your wooden over coat but hat would be too fucking simple. You mad disrespectful, grimy and hard up so I have something better. Ima leave you with something better than dead."

He walks over to the CD player and turns the music up even louder.

"Give me that left hand nigga you just made shit real easy, give me that left hand."

Savius and Major grabbed him up because he was trying to resist. They brought him over to the table and planted his left hand on the table. Prez reaches in the tool box pulls out a roll of duct tape and a pack of firecrackers. He took two firecrackers out the pack and duct taped it between the palms of Mateo's hand. Major and Savius has such a tight grip on him that thru all the fighting, kicking and screaming he can't get loose. Prez took his cigar out the ashtray and lit it.

He took one pull, walked over to Mateo with the butane lighter in his hand with the flicker still going and lit the fire cracker. It exploded in his hand blowing off his index finger and thumb. Mateo screamed so loud he could wake the dead.

Savius immediately got sick and bent over throwing up in the little trash can to the left of him.

"Yo Major, how the fuck Save over there blowing chunks and all his fingers still intact?"

"I don't know he must have a weak stomach or something."

"Call Roof and Raze. Tell em come get this nigga out of here. Drop him in front of hospital. That's the least I can do for a nigga who just tried to kill me right?"

Savius called Roof and Raze; they came to the warehouse to pick Mateo up. Roof has a disgusted look on his face but Raze was steady smiling as he asked.

"Where this nigga going?"

"Drop him in front of Harlem hospital before that nigga die. I aint ready for more blood on my hands than I already have. Lemme holla at him right quick though. Survival is the game, and you put me in this ruthless state of mind, when you walked down Double Cross Road and Deception Street."

"So wear that and I don't wanna ever see you around here again. I could have killed you, but I'd rather you always look at that hand that stole from me, the trigger finger you unsuccessfully squeezed with and remember why you don't have that shit no more. Now get the fuck out of here."

After that day no one ever spoke of what happened. They just went on with their lives as if nothing ever happened. Mateo never came back around. He ended up going down south with his brother Rome. Rome instantly was ready to come back and kill everybody.

Rome was the type that didn't play games when it came to his family, especially his brother. Mateo told him to chill. He didn't want to try and come back right away and retaliate he told him to just lay low for a while and he will decide how he would want to deal with it.

Mateo knew he was wrong for everything he had done to cross Prez and he was more happy to be alive instead of dwelling on losing a couple of fingers. After all, he did steal from Prez and he himself attempted to kill Prez but had no idea that was a movie prop gun. That's when things went downhill.

CHAPTER TWENTY-THREE

The last time Savius spoke to Dana, he felt a cold draft from her. He knew that he hasn't really spending any time with her and this just didn't settle right with him. Dana felt like she was being put on ice and she did want to discuss this with Savius to find out where she stood.

As much as she really wanted and adored him, she did not want to continue on with a hit or miss relationship if it wasn't going to thicken. One morning Savius stopped by her house. He wanted to surprise her with breakfast before she would leave for work. He rang the intercom a few times and he got no answer. He was about to call her on his cell phone when he noticed Dana walking toward the front door. She opens the door.

"What's up Porter baby, for a minute I thought I was gonna have to share this food with the pigeons."

"Hey Save, what you doing here so early in the morning?"

She says with a dry look on her face and sarcastic type of tone.

"I came to have breakfast with you, before you start work."

She changed her tone and her face brightened up.

"That's sweet Savey. You know if it wasn't for my new neighbor Steve, I wouldn't have known you were down here. He knocked on my door to tell me he saw you outside when he was checking his mail. My bell hasn't been working for almost a week now. They're supposed to be fixing it today as a matter of fact. Why didn't you just call?"

"I was about to until I saw the silhouette of your sexiness approaching. Now what's up with this new neighbor? And how he know who I am?"

"He's seen you around here a few times loitering." Dana says while busting out with laughter.

"Is he just a nosey neighbor or is he trying to be overly friendly with Ms. Porter? Cause I don't want to have to put his nose out of joint."

"Save please he's gay so it's not even like that."

"Well in that case he better stop keeping tabs on me. Anyway you just gonna leave me standing here with this food in my hand or are you gonna let me in?"

"My bad Save, here let me take something."

"Nah lady just grab the elevator and we good." They get in the elevator and ride up to the apartment.

"Ooh whatever you have in the bag sure smells great. What is it?"

"Fish, grits, scrambled eggs with cheese of course. Soft buttered rolls, that weird herbal tea you like to drink and ice cold chocolate for me."

"Umm, sounds like I might have to call out from work today. I won't be able to move after a rib sticking meal like that."

"Well that's the idea."

They enter the apartment Dana puts on some soft jazz and sets the table for a romantic candle lit breakfast. They start out with basic conversation, making small talk about nothing in particular as they munch through the meal. Dana was so pleased about the red-letter day they were having so far and wanted to connect with Savius as much she could while she had him there. So without hesitation, she found herself giving her assistant manager Todd a call excusing herself for the day and leaving him in charge of running the shop.

Savius felt he was the man, since he didn't have to pull out his charming power of persuasion to convince Dana into playing hooky from work. Dana wanted to find the right chance to discuss the status of the relationship, but she didn't want to interrupt the relaxing stress free moment they were having, so she decided to put it off until later. They finished breakfast, shared a glass of white wine, talked some more, joked around a bit, equally enjoying one another's company. After placing Dana on cloud nine, Savius puts his feet up and takes a little siesta.

Dana was in seventh heaven; she laid her head down for a little while contemplating the tactic she would use to make Savius understand her feelings and concerns for their relationship. She wrestled with her feelings until she figured out a way to have words with him. Suddenly, the doorbell rings. She wasn't expecting anyone and the bell hasn't worked in days. She leisurely strolls over to the intercom.

"Who is it?"

"It's Mr. Jimmy, is it working okay?"

Mr. Jimmy is the buildings maintenance guy. He was testing the new bell he had just installed. She gave the okay that it was working just fine. She was all set to get back to Savius, and on her way back to the bedroom, she hears a faint knock at the front door. She mutters under her breath.

"Oh boy isn't this freaking great! What now?"

She figured it was Mr. Jimmy coming to bug her since he now knew that she was home. Flinging the door open, with an irritated look on her face, she says out loud.

"What is it now Mr. Jimmy?"

To her surprise, it wasn't Mr. Jimmy. It was her next door neighbor Steve.

"You must be looking at me from a really bad angle if I look like Mr. Jimmy to you." Dana has a dim- witted look on her face.

"Hi Steve, I apologize. I thought you were Mr. Jimmy, he just finished fixing my doorbell and well I know how he can be at times."

"Anything I should know about?"

"He just gets on a roll sometimes, he'll fix one thing, then next thing you know, he's fixing things that are not even broke, and breaking things he can't fix."

"I think he's just trying to make himself useful around here. From what he told me his wife passed away and they did just about everything together, so now he's a lonely man."

"Yeah, that's true. He hasn't been the same since. But he's still a pain in the ass."

"Awl, come on cut the old guy some slack girl. He's just looking to keep busy."

"Yeah, that's true, but it's too early in the day for all that anyway."

"With that being said, I must have come at a bad time."

"No, it's okay. Anyway, how did you know I was still home? And where are you on your way to or coming from looking all sporty?"

Dana says to Steve, while looking him up and down. He had on a gray jogging suit, and the pants were so high up his leg that you couldn't help but to notice the ankle cut Gucci socks he was wearing. He even had the matching headband and wristband. He had on a pair of weight lifting gloves and a pair of old running shoes. Steve was a pretty handsome guy and all, but at the moment he was really out of character. He looked like he was auditioning to be a stunt double in an old Rocky movie or something.

"Well I didn't hear you leave out after I spoke with you this morning, so I was just checking to make sure you were alright. I believe it's my neighborly duty to keep an eye and ear out on things."

"Yeah everything's fine, thank you. I just decided to take the day off."

"Oh ok. Well if you're feeling up for a little run, come on and join me at the park." Dana turns her head and looks over her shoulder.

"Thanks, but I'll take a rain check. I'm in a chill out mood today."

"Are you sure I didn't catch you at a bad time? You seem a bit preoccupied or whatever?"

Before Dana could get the chance to respond, Savius walked up to the front door with a fixed stare on his face and butts in.

"Anytime I'm here, it's a bad time."

"Oh wow, I didn't know you had company."

"Yeah now get lost."

"What?"

"You heard me. Now face the way you came and y'all can finish this girl talk some other time."

"Whoa! What's that supposed to mean?"

Looking him up and down, checking out his whole get up. Savius was about to get into detail about the last comment he made. Dana quickly interrupts.

"Save don't act like that."

"Then tell your lil homo homey bye-bye."

"I guess you feeling a little shaky since you don't come around like you should, but I aint gonna have you punking me like I'm some bitch." Savius steps out into the hallway.

"Oh you a brave little man huh? Unless you looking for a little horror in your life, you better go head before I speckle these walls with your blood."

Mr. Jimmy was peeping down the other end of the hallway while talking to Mr. Little, a tenant who lives on the same floor as Dana and Steve.

"Oh my God!! Steve, please just go I'll talk to you later. Save let it go. You making a scene and I don't need this kind of live drama. You gonna get me kicked out of here."

Steve just walked away for his sake and Dana's. He knew neither one of them could afford to get evicted.

"You know what Dana you right. I'm out; I aint got time to be homeless over some dumb shit."

"Then you'd just be a homeless homo."

What Savius didn't know, is that Dana had lied to him about Steve's sexuality. She figured that by saying Steve was gay, it would make things more acceptable if he ever found out they were hanging out so much.

That cat was surely about to jump out the bag. During the times that Savius wasn't around. Dana and Steve had gone to the movies a few times. Bowling, they went out to eat. They shared the same taste in music and hit up a few jazz clubs, spent time at each other's apartments, playing cards and just kicking back talking. Shit they were practically dating.

Dana would confide in Steve about her feelings and involvement with Savius and would tell him how lonely she was because the time they used to spend together was virtually non-existent. The two started to share an attraction for one another. Although Steve was single and wasn't dating anyone, Dana was still head over heels for Savius, so in her eyes they were keeping things between them on a platonic friendship level.

Steve developed feelings for Dana, but because her feelings were still consumed with Savius, he didn't want to get caught up in a three-way relationship knowing it can all change in a snap of a finger once Savius resurfaces. It's was strange enough that they lived right next door to one another so he fought hard to keep his true feelings for her off the record.

Dana and Savius both re-entered the apartment and an argument begins.

"Save I can't believe you would embarrass me like that."

"Oh! You think I embarrassed you? What about you showin me up chatting it up with your homo homey, while I'm in room waiting for you."

"You know what Save grow up for real."

"You complain about me not spending time with you, I make myself available and you in the hallway playing on my time, with your little girlfriend."

"Why do you have to keep bringing up the fact that he's supposed to be gay?"

"Supposed to be? Either he gay or he's not. Which one is it?"

Dana feels a little nervous because she almost slipped up. She jumped right back in and continued on with her lie.

"Yes, Save the man is gay. But why do you have to keep constantly throwing that out there? It is what it is. I mean you can't possibly feel threatened by him. Or are you?"

"Ha-ha!" Savius laughs.

"Yeah fucking right."

"Then can you just leave it alone? Besides the way you acting is like I'm your girl or something."

Savius didn't utter a word.

"Listen Save, I've been wanting to have this conversation with you for a while now. I didn't want it to be under these circumstances, but since you're here now, I think we should talk about things."

From the bothered expression on Savius's face you can tell this is a conversation he did not want to have.

"Here the fuck we go."

"Can I finish saying what I wanna say?"

"Go ahead."

"I want to know where this is headed. We hardly spend time together. I know you been busy with work, but this is starting to get crazy to me. I'm really feeling you, as a matter of fact, I'm crazy about you and we been seeing each other for a minute so I don't want to just throw it all away."

No matter which way Dana conveyed her feelings to Save, he automatically jumped on the defense because he wasn't ready to have this conversation.

"Dana, Hold up! Freeze right there. From the jump, I never spoke to you with a silver tongue."

Dana interrupts.

"So what. What you telling me? That I been wasting my time?"

"I never told you to hold your breath and wait for me. I thought you understood that we were on the chill, but now all of a sudden you trying to flip it up."

"After all the time we put in are you saying you don't give a fuck about me?"

"That's how you feel?"

"Yes, Save that's how I feel. Now answer the question."

"So if you think I don't give a fuck about you, then why you coming at me with all of this and why am I here?"

"I don't know you tell me. Maybe to bang me down and go."

"Bang you down and go? You sound mother fucker stupid as hell right now. If that was the case, I would have been done that. We may not spend all the time that you obviously want and you know why. I aint about to mix up business for pleasure. Did that already and it almost fucked me up."

Since the last time Savius and Prez faced off, he wasn't feeling that at all and now that Mateo is no longer in the picture his work load basically doubled. So the time he was juggling between work and chilling with Dana did go interrupted but for now his back was against the wall and he had to do what he had to do.

"Listen Save, all I'm saying is that I'm not getting any younger, shit I want to have at least once kid and get married one day. Is it a crime to want the things I see that other people have?"

"I don't make it my business to want what I see other people have. I make it my business to want what I want."

"I'm saying look at Prez and Khandi. I see that fat ass sparkler he put on her finger. They working towards making things happen. Why can't that be us?"

"Be us what? So let me ask you this. You chasing the diamond or all the serious shit that comes behind that? And you really out your lane talking rings and shit. Come on girl! Khandi and Prez been together since they were kids. Are you kidding me or what? And stop tryna keep up with someone else. No better yet stop tryna keep up with Khandi. I thought you were your own person, better yet I thought you were more advanced than that."

She stood there with a blank look on her face and didn't respond to the fact that he called her on trying to copy Khandi. She's heard enough of that from Donna.

"Time has nothing to do with it."

"So if time has nothing to do with it, why you rushing me into something that's very far from my reach anyway?"

"Because if you love somebody, throw caution to the wind."

Savius was taken back and has this dazed look on his face.

"Yes, you heard me. I love you. Aren't you gonna say it back?"

"What you want me say huh? What you want me to do huh? Rub you down with snake oil and tell you all the shit you wanna hear?"

"Wow."

"Fuck you wowing about?"

"You know what Save, You wrong, I don't need you telling me shit I just wanna hear, only shit that's real and shit just got real without you even saying much. So you know what boo boo, just go."

"So you throwin me out?"

"No you did that to yourself."

"Alright cool, I got you. You aint gonna have this nigga walking round with invisible handcuffs."

Dana is more hurt and disappointed and Savius is more upset and pig headed. He grabs up his belongings and slams the door on his way out.

CHAPTER TWENTY-FOUR

After several weeks and no contact with Savius, Dana had come to realize that she would eventually take the bull by the horns and deal with the hard-hitting reality that perhaps she and Savius were not going to be together.

Ever since the verbal altercation between Dana and Savius she was feeling a little depressed. So by the end of week she decided to get out and clear her head by doing a little shopping. On her way out the door she ran into Steve.

"Hey Dana, how you been? You look like you just lost your best friend or something."

"It sure feels that way. You know me and Save beefing right now."

"That's too bad." Steve responds with complete phoniness in his voice.

"But hey you still have me."

"Thanks Steve that's sweet of you."

"So where you headed to looking all cute and shit?"

"I'm about to go and do what girls do, when they feeling a little down."

"You must be going to spend some money." Steve says while chuckling.

"Yes. How did you know?"

"Cause like you said, that's what girls do. So where are you going to clean out your bank account?"

"Macy's down on 34th Street."

"What a twist of fate. I was planning on going there come Saturday. I'm almost out of cologne and was going to go cop a new bottle. Mind if I tag along? Besides you look like you can use the company?"

"Not a bad idea."

"Give me ten minutes while I run upstairs, change clothes and get my wallet."

"Don't run, just walk I'll be right here soaking up some of this beautiful sun."

"You do know that's just a saying right?"

"You do know that was a joke right?" They both start laughing.

"Now hurry up run go get your wallet." They catch a cab over to 34th street.

"Wait Steve, I want to get a pretzel and soda first. I feel like being bad today. I never could resist those things." Dana says while sniffing the aroma in the air.

"Yeah, I can go for dirty water myself."

"Dirty water? Steve what are you talking about?" Steve laughs.

"Oh yeah I can tell you're not a native New Yorker. Dirty water is what we call the hotdogs from the cart."

"Never thought of it in that sense. Yuck."

They stop and get their pretzel, hotdog and soda before going inside Macy's. Once they were done, they make their way inside and begin to look around. After some time has passed, they separate. Steve goes over to the Calvin Klein section of the store while Dana is on the other side looking around. All of a sudden she hears a familiar voice and she looks up.

"Well, well, well. If it isn't good old Clarence."

"Excuse me?"

"Well after all you are standing here obviously counting your pennies on the clearance rack aren't you? So yeah, I'll scratch out Dana and just call you Clarence for now on, it suites you better."

"Get a life."

"Don't get mad because you got busted. See the Dana that everybody else knows wouldn't get caught dead digging in the clearance rack trying to find fashion at a bargain price."

"First of all I'm here shopping with a friend."

Dana says as she continues to sort through the racks of clothing.

"See you real quick on a lie. Let me show you an example of what truth sounds like. I'm here shopping for myself, looking for a cute little birthday get up. Now Dana tell me was that hard?"

"Actually, I'm not interested in why you're here."

"But I'm sure Khandi will be interested to know why her basement bargain copy- cat fake friend is here swiveling thru the racks."

"Well how about I tell her that since she had already mentioned you have a birthday coming up, I was trying to find something suitable for your taste. You know cheap and outdated."

"Is this the same person that lives in a house where there isn't enough room to even swing a cat?"

"You know what Donna, you're childish. So why don't you run along. But then again I can understand why you're so simple. Aren't you a leap year baby? Which means you're always four years behind yourself so how can I expect you to keep up with me?"

Steve walks up with a concerned look on his face. He caught the tail end of their little confrontation.

"Hey Dana, are you ready to go?"

Donna's eyes and mouth stretched wide open with surprised when she caught sight of Steve, she now had two things to go run back and tell. Dana was unmoved; she turned to Donna and blows her a kiss.

"I'm ready Steve. And Donna, Mwah! Smooches."

She and Steve walk off. Steve looks back at Donna like she had just committed a crime.

CHAPTER TWENTY-FIVE

That same night during a card game at Prez and Khandi's house, Donna struck up distasteful conversation with Savius.

"Hey Save! You seem to be in the pink these days since you handed Dana your notice. That's a good thing. I happened to see her earlier today and other than poor fashion sense, she seems to be a little jolly with her new dude. I tell you, girls like that don't waste much time."

Everyone got silent, fixing their eyes on Donna like she had just broken the ultimate veil of secrecy. He sat there sorting thru his hand of cards looking lost in thought, like Donna had just dug out a piece of his heart. He looked up at Donna and just threw his hands in the air.

"Oh please it must feel good breaking those chains."

Prez knew that Savius had more feelings for Dana than he cared to admit, so he steps in and says a thing or two to Donna.

"Yo Donna, when you gonna learn to keep your tongue in your cheek? Worry about your own shit and leave my man's alone."

"I'm just calling it like I know. Dana was trying to take him prisoner, build up stocks, and carbon copy Khandi. But I saw the cheap tramp in Macy's shopping on the clearance rack and she was with a dude."

"Okay, so she values her money."

"That's a nice way of putting it."

"And you don't know who that man could have been."

"They looked pretty cozy, I'll tell you that. Some nigga named Steve."

"Yo Dee, Why you bringing my man to court at a card game?"

"Because she had everybody hoodwinked but I already knew what she was all about."

"Yo Donna, pull in your horns, and have a seat." He starts laughing at Donna.

"Even I Know who Steve aint nothing. So let me recap on this. You came here to let us know that Dana shops on a budget with her flaming boyfriend slash girlfriend Steve. Ok now have a seat and we'll just try to forget that you just made an ass out of yourself once again."

Khandi didn't want the fire to erupt between Prez and Donna so she stepped in.

"You should have been a broadcaster because you love putting things on air.

"WOW! For real Khandi?" Donna replied with a hurt tone in her voice.

"Yes Donna for real. There's a time and place for things. Now is not the time, nor the place. Prez is right you need to know when to keep your tongue in your cheek."

Prez wasn't feeling all the words bouncing back and forth over Savius's head so he gets at Donna one last time.

"Yo Dee, I'm giving you the elbow anyway, you not even a paying player at this table. The only thing you pay is attention to is shit that doesn't concern you, fuck around and make me call my Man Chuck on ya ass."

"You know what." Before she could complete her next sentence Prez cuts her off.

"Everlasting lip service. Why don't you go fan your flames and come back with a different frame of mind? You know talk about some useful shit."

"Alright Prez, you got it. But let me say one last thing to Save then my shit is sealed." She walks behind Savius and wraps her arms around his shoulders.

"Save you know we cool and I just want to see you treated right and she aint right."

Prez steps in again.

"Donna is you fucking kidding me?"

Savius cuts him off.

"Nah its cool dog let her speak."

"Anyway, like I was saying, keep that fork in the road and you'll thank me later. Trust me, I'm right on this. You need to holler at Chloe anyway, she been crushing on you for a long time."

Prez starts laughing.

"Now you a matchmaker Dee?"

Donna is feeling like everyone is taking a dim view of her so she decides to leave.

As soon as he walks off, Solomon gets up from the table.

"It's getting real narrow in here, yo Swift man let's bounce."

"Yeah, you right, Khandi your crony definitely knows how to put on a floor show. I hope I never let any debts go unpaid with her cause I know she'll discredit a nigga just on some loose change."

Solomon butts in.

"Discredit? Na dog, more like open fire on a nigga. But if you ask me, I think she has the green eyes for Dana and she might even be a little warm hearted for Save."

"Take notes, it's more like a little of both ya heard. Yo Prez spot you later."

After some time passed, everyone else starts to fade out. Khandi goes upstairs and retires for the night. Prez and Savius are the only two left standing. Prez wanted to have a word with Savius. Prez walks behind the wet bar.

"What you drinking?"

"Give me a shot of Hennessey." Prez pours him and Savius a shot.

"Let's take the weight off our shoulders and chinwag for a minute."

"Alright what's up?"

"You seemed to be in a tight corner with Donna backbiting Dana."

"I just let her rock cause you know how it sometimes you just wanna keep your personal hap under wraps and Donna has a problem respecting that at times."

"Word up."

"She'll put the spotlight on a motherfucker in a heartbeat and make shit public notice."

"Word up."

Prez throws back another shot and pours Savius another.

"She knows that's not how I flow. That's just why I didn't piggy back that shit."

"True that. But you know what Save between me and you right now, I think you have more zeal for Dana than you letting up on."

"She cool, we was chillin you know having fun or whatever until she started letting her hair down. Aint nothing."

"Yo Save, I know you like the back of my hand my dude. You fighting hard not to respond to something that you really feel deep inside, just know that if it's real it's not gonna just go away."

"Everything was good until she wanted to touch shoulders with a nigga and you see where that got me."

"That's why you gotta balance your shit out that's all. Me and Khandi do it and we good. Why can't you and Dana?"

"Now here you go."

"Listen, you can try and dupe me and everyone else around you, but you can't dupe yourself."

There was an awkward moment of silence. Prez pours another shot of Henny and refills Savius's glass as well. Savius throws back the shot and he sits there in a quick daze, with his head down.

"Yo, I didn't see this whole thing coming. I laid it all down from day one and I let myself go. I aint recognize I felt that love for her until after I gave her the chop. She really did play an important role in my life. Since we haven't been together I learned to have a certain type of appreciation for her that I didn't have before. I didn't think I would be saying this so soon, but I love that girl."

"You have to go see her and close the gap. Let her know how you feel."

"I messed that up being hard- nosed. Too much time done passed. I just have to take that loss."

"I disagree, as much as that girl tried making you her man, do you really think that if you stepped to her with your heart basically in your hand she would turn her back on you? Dana would turn to liquid cause she still got mad love for you. Reach her now before she puts you down as another experience."

Savius goes home, and later that night he contemplated long and hard about the advice that Prez had given him. It was a restless night he couldn't seem to clear his head, so he picked up the phone and called Dana. Much to his surprise she had changed her number. He called 411 to get her new number and it was non-published. This left him with only two other ways to try and contact her. He would have to stop by her house or visit her at the job. He wasn't feeling either or because he didn't know if Dana would give a positive response to him.

If they were still together it almost mark a year from the time they met. Dana's birthday was coming up toward the end of the week and he at least wanted to wish her a happy birthday. He stopped by her job the next day. He figured if he saw her there, she would be held in reserve.

Dana was at the rear of the store helping a customer when Savius walked in. he waited patiently as he admired her from afar. Dana had a way about her that allowed her to hold a man's attention with no problem. She took notice of him and instantly had this mystified expression on her face as she slowly walked towards him.

"Hello Ms. Porter."

"Hey Save, what are you doing here?"

"I need to talk to you. I called your phone and you changed your number I see."

"What is this about Save?"

"I know it's been a minute and you probably have ill feelings for me and I deserve that. But I at least need to clear the air cause I don't like the way we left things between us."

"Don't you mean the way you left things between us?"

"Dana don't make this too hard on a nigga, that's not what I'm here for."

"Look Save if your days are filled with guilt and you're expecting me to tell you all the things you want to hear, just so you don't have to feel bad about moving on with your life then you're wrong."

"I kind of expected this. I'm willing to listen to whatever you have to say, but I don't want to just stand here and rattle off. Can we meet up later?"

"Damn Save, even after all that was said and done, I'm not capable of slapping your face and casting you to hell. I still love you and wanted you to feel the same way to. But I learned that no matter how much feelings, you may have for a person, you can't make them feel the same way about you. I'm still willing to hear you out. I close shop at 7 tonight meet me at my house by 9 and we can talk over dinner."

"How about a birthday dinner?"

"My birthday isn't till the end of the week. You know that."

"I know that but just in case you're not feeling things or feeling me, I can at least celebrate with you tonight."

"Save you know I'm superstitious and I don't celebrate anything before it's time."

"Okay then we'll just have dinner."

Savius exits the shop and commences to prepare for the first class evening he felt Dana ought to have. Once he gets in his car he picks up his mobile phone and calls in dinner reservations at Giovanni's. After dinner he plans to take Dana to Gee's, a nice little jazz club downtown that she likes to go to.

Next he calls CAS One car service and rents a ride to transport the around for the entire evening. He wants to make sure that all of his attention is geared toward Dana and if all goes well, the last thing he wants to do is keep his eyes on the road and hands on the steering wheel. He stops by Kaseam's to get a quick shape up while chatting with some of the old timers for a short while. Just as he was headed out the front door his cell phone goes off. It's an urgent text message from Donna, asking him to call her at home. He is not up for any drama today so he turns his cell off and heads home.

CHAPTER TWENTY-SIX

Meanwhile back at Prez and Khandi's house, Donna has managed to bring drama all over again. She had it in for Dana ever since day one when the two first met. Donna stayed determined that she would at some point in time expose the true person that in her eyes Dana would eventually turn out to really be.

The final war came after the last war of words between Donna, Khandi and the rest of her closest friends. Which now have become drifting has-beens. Donna has never been the type of person to do things halfway so she contacted Hermels's, a Private Detective agency owned by two brother's Herman and Melvin Gray located downtown Brooklyn. She paid top dollar, to let them do the probing for her. Within two weeks, they got to the nitty-gritty and brought things to the light. The investigation was thorough enough to bring more than enough information that would once and for all confirm that Donna was right concerning her suspicions when it came to Dana.

Donna was so anxious to present the evidence that Dana was not exactly the person she portrayed herself to be. She couldn't let even another minute pass by to reveal this fake life Dana was walking around paying claim to. She called s Savius on his cell phone and mobile phone countless times, but got no answer.

She drove over to Prez and Khandi's house thinking he would be there. Donna was so pumped up that when she got to the house, she jumped out the car leaving the driver's side door open and the engine still running, frantically pressing the doorbell and hammering on the front door so hard it seemed like she was about to bring the house down. Prez and Khandi are awaked from an afternoon nap. Prez reaches in the nightstand drawer pulling out his 9mm. He reacted so quickly because he thought shit was about to go down.

He turns on the remote surveillance camera in the bedroom and catches sight of Donna.

"Yo, what the fuck!"

"I got it baby; let me go see what's up."

Prez is tight from being startled out his sleep and when he realized it was Donna he wasn't beat because lately she's been coming with the drama. So Khandi goes downstairs first to see to what was going on. The moment Khandi opens the front door, Donna rushes her way through yelling out.

"I got it; I got it all on paper! Black and white. Where's Save? Ooh he is gonna hit the fucking roof. Ooh! Ooh! Ooh! He won't be able to close his eyes to this one!"

"Donna what are you talking about? And how you gonna leave your car wide open with the engine running?"

"Oh shit be right back."

She goes outside and properly parks her car and comes back inside, "Girl you crazy, now what's this you talking about?"

"What am I talking about? What am I talking about? Ha-ha! I'm talking about this right here, black and fucking white. I need to see Save."

Donna is wound up pacing the floors, waving some papers around in her hand.

"I need to see Save."

"First of all Dee, Save is not here and just by the way you're carrying on, I'm thankful that he's not. Now spill it, what is this about?"

"We need to sit down for this one Khandi Girl. First pour me a little drinky drink."

Khandi knows that it's much too early to get Donna started with drinking because she knows how she can get. But she figured that, with the way Donna was all wound up, this could be the thing to calm her down a little. She goes down to the basement and comes back with a shot of absolute on the rocks and hands it to Donna. Donna swigs it down so fast all you can hear was the ice clanging in the bottom of the glass. They walk into the dining room and take a seat. Donna hands Khandi the papers she was waving around and she begins to read.

Hermels Private Eye

Investigation Report

Type: Background Check

Case #: 12221968

Subject Name: Dana Porter

Results: Complete

Date: June 20th 2002

Dana Niche Porter: Born June 24th 1977

Birthplace: Boston City Hospital, Boston MA

Education: High School Graduate, Boston College High school

Designer Institute: Incomplete

Marital Status: Divorced/ married one year and six months

EX Husband: Phillip Justice/ Jazz musician

Children: one child born within the marriage. Deana Justice aged 5 born without sight/ Attends Perkins School for the blind – Boston, MA.

Parents: Julian and Janet Porter

Parents Occupation: Father: Ultrasound Technician at St. Brandon's Hospital/Mother: Tailor at Blanches dry cleaners Boston Ma.

Notes: Ms. Porter voluntarily signed all parental rights over to the child's birth father. As a result she has no communication with her ex-husband, or her child. She consistently makes monthly donations to The Perkins School for the blind. Ms. Porter presently resides in New York City, working for the Ralph Lauren store downtown. Manhattan. She is recently enrolled in the Fashion Institute of Technology, due to start in September.

Khandi finishes reading the document. She is visibly shaken by what she just read. She is disappointed in what she just learned and even more so at the fact that Savius is not going to take this news too well.

"Damn, Dee, now I need a drink."

She goes downstairs and comes back up with Crystal decanter filled with Bushmill's Irish whiskey. She Pours she and Donna a straight shot and they chug it down like it was water.

"Dee, I don't know what to say right now. It's obvious you were right when you said Dana was putting on fronts about things. Save is gonna be broke up because he is really feeling that girl. Shit she had me fooled. I can't believe she actually has a child and was married before that's the part I can't wrap my head around more than anything. I sat down on many occasions telling her so much of my business and she was sitting there taking me on fantasy flights. And damn Dee you mean to tell me that you was so content that you spent money on this?"

"No. Correction, Chuckey's money."

"Dee you are a something else."

"Yeah, well whatever I am, I'm the real deal. Anyway, Good thing Save gave that bitch the boot though"

"Not so fast, he's actually trying to get back with her. He finally opened up about how he really feels for her and he made all these plans to win her back."

"Win her back?"

Donna loudly kisses her teeth

"Like she some fucking prize. Anyway where is Save? I have to show him this before I explode. And where's Prez?"

Khandi was gone for a while, so Prez comes downstairs to find out what the ruckus was about anyway.

"Right here under your nose. Don't tell me you lost your sense of smell. You sniff everything else what's the problem?"

"Prez trust me this is not a good time for the jokes."

"This better be good Dee, cause you was about to get owned. Out there pounding dents in my door. This better be fucking good."

"I'm here because I need to show something very important to Save.

"I know you have a better chance of reaching him than I do."

"Right now you don't need to be dropping no lines to my Dog. Haven't you delivered enough low blows?"

"Prez you need to hear her out on this."

"I'm sure it's about her little hobby horse Dana. But if it isn't some official shit, then it's nothing! You heard?"

Donna picks up the paper and hands it over to Prez.

"This time it's all in black and white, just read it."

Prez takes a look at the paperwork. After he's done reading it he turns to Donna, basically expressionless.

"Well, I guess you won the cutthroat competition after all."

"Prez that's not fair, I mean am I wrong for trying to look out for a good friend?"

"Is this shit authentic? Or some shit you put together to prove a point?"

"Me and Chucky hired the P.I."

Prez cuts her off, "Nah, Dee, see that's where you fucked up. My man Chuck aint getting involved in no shit like this."

"Okay, but he gave me the money."

"You lying and shit you want me to believe what you telling me at the same time."

"Okay, let me start over. Chucky gave me the money for me to do whatever and this is what I did. You can call the PI yourself, if you really don't believe me. But you can be for sure that every bit of it is real."

"Nothing is for sure but death and taxes. I'm gonna ask you again. Is this official shit or what?"

"Yes. It's official."

"Then in that case Dee, I have to respect that you saw the writing on the wall. I never put energy into the situation because I figured it would just fizzle out anyway. But I know my dog is in deeper than just his ankles, so I'm gonna go light on my approach."

"Yeah, Prez we know that you deal with some with a cold hand, but when it comes to friends and family you have a warm heart."

Donna says laughing while turning in Khandi's direction.

"Khandi girl you haven't said a word in the last ten minutes?"

"I'm just thinking about Save and how will face all of this. I'm also thinking about how Save would have responded to you. The two of you would be throwing spit right now. You were all amped up and I know you mean well but Dee you have to consider the other person's feelings when you're bringing bad or difficult news."

"Yeah Donna, you got to be easy. It's not always the issues you bring; it's how you bring it."

"I guess I was hyped out because I finally had hard copy prove my point. I had been trying for a long time let y'all see through this girl. There was something there from day one and I couldn't let it go you know what I mean Prez?"

“More like wouldn’t let it go, but I hear you.”

“I understand what y’all saying though. So can I be put back on the friends and family plan now?”

Donna stands there with her arms stretched out giving Prez and Khandi a big hug. Prez stands there with his hand clasped on his chin, shaking his head with a ruined look on his face.

“Damn man, Save put a lot of planning into the royal evening ahead. I can’t botch that up tonight. I’m gonna let it rock tonight but tomorrow I’m breaking the news.”

Khandi and Donna both agree.

CHAPTER TWENTY-SEVEN

Savius picked Dana up and she was impressed from the start of the date. Everything went as planned to the Tee. Dana felt like the happiest woman alive and Savius felt like the luckiest man alive. They were feeling each other just as they did the very first day they met. Dana couldn't seem to wipe that smile off her face once Savius threw caution to the wind and actually looked her in the eyes and told her how much he really does loves her. She spent the night at Savius's house and in the morning she met Ms. Lexi. She knew at that point shit was real.

On Savius's way dropping Dana back home, he gets a call from Prez. With his earplugs in his ear he takes the call. The way he answered the phone you can tell he had his happy voice back.

"What's up Bro?"

"Driving with one hand on the steering wheel and holding Dana's hand with the other." Prez didn't want to upset him while he was driving so he tried to sound like everything was normal.

"Waddup Save? Where you at right now?"

"I'm headed to the city, dropping my baby home."

Dana and Savius look over at one another cheesin mad hard.

"Oh alright, listen stop by the house when you done doing that."

"Alright."

"Alright, One."

He hangs up with Prez and he and Dana start talking.

"Who was that Prez?"

"Yeah, he wants me to stop by the house. I know he wanna know how our night went. I'll give him that."

"Don't give him too much though. I won't be able to look him in the eye next time I see him."

Dana starts laughing, "Oh, you funny. Why not? You don't want him to know how you put it down and put a nigga to sleep last night?"

"Save you embarrassing me now."

"Nah we don't get down like that, besides he already knows. I'm whipped and it aint over nothing."

Dana is blushing so hard; she is almost too bashful to look back at him. So to bring her back when they got to the traffic light he leaned over and asked for a kiss. They kissed and were so into one another that the light had turned green and they were still sitting there kissing until the other drivers in traffic started blowing their horns. He drops Dana home and heads over to Prez and Khandi's house.

He gets to the house and rings the bell, Khandi lets him in.

"Hey Save how you doing? Why didn't you just use your key?"

"I guess I aint wanna catch y'all two in here doing the nasty?"

"That's what the bedroom is for silly."

"I'm sure y'all done tore up almost every room in this house already." They start laughing.

"Can you tell I'm in a good mood?"

"Mm mm Hmmmm."

Khandi quickly cuts him off sending him downstairs to Prez because she knows what's about to happen and she doesn't want to keep things going because pretty soon Savius is going to be more than pissed when he hears what's coming next.

"What's up Prezo?"

Savius walks over to the refrigerator with a smooth swag in his step, grabs an ice cold beer, pops the cap and throws it back.

"Yo, my Nigga, last night." Prez interrupts in a hurry.

"Yo Save take a seat man, we need to talk real talk."

"What happened now? I miss one day of work and some bullshit went down?"

"Well yeah and no."

"What do you mean?"

"Well this aint about business, this is personal." Savius looks confused.

"Okay, what's wrong?"

"It's Dana yo."

"Dana? What about Dana?"

"Well Donna." Savius cuts him short.

"Not this Donna shit again yo, I can't I'm gonna flip cause."

Savius is getting hyped up, pushing his palms in the air, doing a little two step.

"Save!"

Prez calls out with a loud but serious tone in his voice. He takes out the paper and sets it on the table.

"Just read this."

"What's this?"

"Just read it."

He starts to read over the paper. When he was finished he just sat there a long while without uttering a single word. He sat there like every bit of life had been drained from him. Prez sat there in silence as well. Khandi was upstairs on standby, just in case Prez needed her because they really didn't know how he was going to take the disappointing news.

Donna called Khandi to find out how Save reacted to the news as well. Khandi answers the phone with a faint whisper in her voice.

"Hello?"

"What happened, is he going off?"

"No. but I don't hear anything, it's quiet down there."

"Oh, where they at? In the basement or something?"

"Aint no something Donna, yes they're in the basement."

"So why they not talking?"

"I don't know."

"Donna, I know why I'm whispering, but what the hell are you whispering for?"

"Oh, true." Laughing.

"Look Donna, I'm hanging up. I'll call you back when I know something."

"Okay." Donna responds while still whispering.

"Shaking my head and you still whispering, girl you a trip bye!"

As soon as Khandi hangs up the phone she starts to hear voices.

"Prez where did you get this from?"

"Donna."

"Yo, here we go again."

"It's official though, I think you need to go holler at Dana, see what this is all about cause it aint looking too good."

"Yeah, I'm on it."

"You alright Dog? You, wanna talk about this?"

With a crackled tone in his voice, Savius responds.

"Nah, I just need to get to the bottom of this. I just poured myself out to this girl last night and now this? Listen I can't even talk about this right now. I'm out. I'll hit you later."

Savius leaves Prez and Khandi's house and heads straight over to Dana's. Once he got outside and was in the car alone his anger started to erupt. He started driving really fast, punching the steering wheel, blasting his music really loud and even running a couple of red lights. He was really a mess at this point.

He gets to Dana's house, rings the bell and she buzzes him in.

"Hey baby, I wasn't expecting you back so quick."

Standing on her tippy toes she leans in with her lips puckered up to give him a kiss. He stormed passed her so fast that she lost her balance.

"Save what's wrong baby?"

Savius takes the paper and hands it to her.

"Tell me this bullshit Dana."

She looks at the paper and starts to read it. Her hands start to shake uncontrollably.

"Oh My God! Save where did you get this from? You hired a private eye on me?"

"No, but Donna did. All I want to know is if this is true."

He is yelling so loud that he scares Dana and she jumps.

"Save calm down you're scaring me. Yes it's true, let me explain.

Her eyes are filled with tears and she starts to cry.

"After I graduated from high school, my parents didn't have enough money to send me to fashion and design school. So I got a job and started working at an animal shelter in order to save enough money to follow my dreams. Well shortly after, I started seeing this guy. We started getting close and I ended up pregnant. At first I wasn't going to keep the baby, but he convinced me to keep it, promised to marry me so we can be a family and he would help me in every way possible to continue my dreams so I can advance into a career in fashion. So I agreed and we got married."

By this time tears are pouring down her face and she is still visibly shaken.

"The pregnancy was pretty tough in the beginning, so he wanted me to quit my job at the animal shelter. Instead of quitting, I cut down my hours and started working part time. Anyway, time went on, things seemed to be going well. But I was young and dumb, only 18 and thought I knew it all. With that being said, I really didn't keep up with all my doctor's appointments like I should have. I end up getting sick over time and I chose to ignore things because I figured those were the things that went along with being pregnant. I would get headaches, muscle pains and even a little blurred vision at times. Well the baby was born premature and she was under 5lbs. other than that, things seemed to be fine. Well my illness symptoms didn't really go away after I had her and I chalked it up to post pregnancy stress until I actually had a seizure. The doctors ran test and could find anything wrong. But then the baby started taking on some of the same symptoms that I was experiencing. Her major symptom when she had turned a year old was Chorioretinitis which is inflammation of the eyes which can lead to blindness and in her case it did just that. The doctors ran test on both me and the baby and they found that we had something called Toxoplasmosis. The doctors narrowed things down and found that I had contracted this illness from working at the animal shelter, carelessly handling contaminated cat soil. I immediately blamed myself and the more time passed by so did he. Things had gotten really terrible between us, so much so that we decided to get a divorce."

Savius interrupts.

"Baby I'm sorry."

"No Save let me finish please; I didn't feel I was fit enough as a mother to raise a child, especially one with a disability and one that I felt totally responsible for. As much as we disagreed on everything else, that's the one thing we both came into agreement with. He convinced me to sign over my parental rights and leave quietly. I really didn't fully understand the ramifications of my actions. Like I said before, I was young and if I didn't mention, he was quite a few years older than me. My family was so upset with me and seeing my father cry for the 1st time in all my life and the way he cried, killed me inside. My ex-husband end up flipping things on me and made it look as if I did it for selfish reasons because I wanted to pursue a career and make it all about me and that just wasn't the truth. Things got so intense and ugly between us including with my own family that one day I just packed my things and left. I always had plans on going back to get my daughter, but once the time was right, once I was right. As you can see here on this paper I always donate to her school, because after all that has happened that's the least I can do. I've tried countless times reaching out but no one would talk to me. Save this is why I declined telling you because I couldn't afford to have you thinking less of me to and keep scaling over a wound that would probably never heal."

Savius grabs her up and holds her tight in his arms, telling her everything was going to be okay. He even went as far to tell her that he was going to help her get her daughter back. This was a tear jerking moment and between them two, there wasn't a dry eye in the house.

Their relationship went on untouched. Savius explained everything to Khandi and Prez and they both felt Dana's pain. They were able to bypass the other little foolish tales she told and they were ready to move passed it all. This situation actually strengthened their bond and they were in love more than ever. Dana's birthday was coming up in the next two days, so Save wanted to do something special for her, something a little more intimate. He ordered an expensive bottle of Champagne, cake and roses. He got Ms. Lexi to make a pan of shrimp scampi, one of Dana's favorite dishes. He planned on surprising her when she would come home from work and have everything set up and ready to put a smile on her face.

It's noon on the day Dana's birthday. Savius paid Mr. Jimmy $100.00 to let him into the apartment so he can set up shop. He hadn't spoken to her all day and assumed that she was at work. He did hit her up with a happy birthday text and told her they can do something later when she gets off work and she agreed. He decorated the room with a dozen balloons, candles, rose petals from the threshold to the bedroom, a banner neatly taped on the bedroom; wall that read, "I love you." It was quite a romantic scene.

He lays across the bed patiently awaits her arrival. He decided to smoke a blunt to pass time and help him relax a little. He misplaced his lighter so he fumbled through her bedside table trying to find matches so he can light his blunt. He smokes the blunt and watches a little television. He forgot to sign the birthday card that he brought for her so he fumbles back around in the bedside table. He notices her journal which had a pen stuck within the pages. He opens the journal and what he caught sight of was something that instantly changed his outlook on everything between him and Dana's relationship.

Dear Journal,

I am in a confused state right now. I feel bad because I have been lying to Savius about my relationship with my next door neighbor Steve. Steve and I had become very close during the times I felt neglected and abandoned by Savius. I wasn't sure if me and Savius were even going to make it. I poured out my heart to him and told him how I felt and in return I got nothing. We went almost a month with no communication and then one day he pops up at my job wanting to work things out. I did lie to him and I told him that Steve was gay. I did this because I didn't want Savius giving me problems about me and Steve hanging out. At first it was all innocent but then in Savius's absence Steve and I did become very close and our bond got strong. Well now that me and Save are back together and planning on building the

relationship I always wanted, I have to find a way to let Steve down easy. I made things complicated and I take full responsibility for it because I never should have slept with Steve knowing my emotions were still so very high, and my heart was still big for Save.

Savius is so upset that a feeling rushed through his body like he just wanted to kill something. He wanted to pick up the phone and call somebody but he decided not to. He was a little embarrassed because he did so much to fight against a serious relationship with this woman, to then turn around and fight so hard to be in a relationship with this woman who has now turned his life upside down.

He paces the floors waiting for her to come home. He's so hot right now; that it feels like his blood is practically boiling. He feels like just going down to her job and confronting her right there on the spot but he decided to just wait. A couple of hours go by and he hears voices in the hallway, one of which was Dana's. He eagerly waited for her to open the apartment door so he can confront her. Instead he hears the door next door open and close. He can clearly hear laughter from the other side of the wall. He wasn't about to be played a fool not even a minute longer.

He puts on his shoes, tears the page out of the journal and shoves it in his back pocket. He walks out in the hallway and starts pouncing on Steve's door.

Bang Bang Bang!

"What the fuck." Steve responds.

"Open the fucking door motherfucker."

Dana and Steve both looked confused.

"Save?"

Dana calls out with a fearful tone in her voice.

"Dana, handle your business or I will. This asshole must be stupid banging on my door like that."

Dana goes over to the door and swings it wide open.

"So you and your little fake as homo friend been playing me huh?"

"Save what are you talking about? You need to calm down."

"Calm down? Calm down? Did you just fucking say that I need to calm down?" Steve butts in.

"Yo I don't know what's going on right now and I aint interested. Take this mess next door or wherever you need to be."

Savius starts pushing his way through the door.

"Fuck you just say to me nigga?"

"Save stop you being stupid right now"

"Oh I'm being stupid huh? Well how about this; let's see if this is stupid to you."

He reaches towards his back pocket to pull out the paper he tore out from the journal. In a quickness Steve yelled out.

"Oh hell no."

He reaches under his mattress and pulls out a gun. Dana turns around and she jumps in front of Savius yelling out no!!

Savius pulls out the paper at the same time one shot rang out and Dana hits the floor. She is bleeding so much that her whole shirt was covered in blood. For a second everyone is in total shock. Savius grabs Dana, holding her lifeless body in his arms.

"See what the fuck you just did? Call 911 motherfucker. Come on baby please, don't be dead! You can't die on me. Come on baby wake up!"

"911? Yes I need an ambulance to I shot someone and I think she might be dead!" Steve places the gun on the kitchen table and calmly takes a seat waiting for the cops to come.

Savius is crying so hard and he is shaking so badly but he won't let her go. The cops and EMS enter the building and make their way up to the apartment. The EMS move Savius out of the way and immediately start to work on Dana. The cops asked questions about what just happened. They took the gun and placed it in a plastic bag. They took a statement from both Steve and Savius. Steve is read his Miranda rights, handcuffed and arrested. The EMS tried everything to revive Dana but it was too late and she didn't make it. Savius called Prez and Khandi and they drove over to the apartment to get him. They contacted Dana's family and told them about what has happened. Her family made it to New York the very next morning. They had Dana's body transported back to Boston where funeral services were held.

CHAPTER TWENTY-EIGHT

Two weeks had passed following Dana's untimely death. Savius had remained in a depressed state of mind and justifiably so. He spent a lot of time locked away in his bedroom with the curtains drawn closed; sleeping most of the time and when he was awake he would just turn up a bottle and drink enough to force himself back to sleep. Ms. Lexi had become concerned that this temporary psychological state was lingering far too long. I mean she did expect that he would go through his grieving process, but she didn't foresee him shutting out his close circle of friends and especially not her. He blocked out all outside communication by keeping his cell phone turned off and advising his Mother he didn't want any visitors.

Ms. Lexi and Savius were always very close. It was always the two of them ever since his Father was deported back to Panama when he was a young child. She and Savius were always able to talk about anything, but things were changing right before her eyes and the bottles of alcohol and messy California King sized bed had now become his bosom buddy. One evening he staggered off to bed in a drunken stupor and he hadn't eaten all day. Ms. Lexi had prepared one of his favorite meals and she commenced to bring it to his bedroom.

She knocked on the door. Knock, Knock

There was no answer.

She knocked on the door a couple more times and called out to him.

"Pappy." A nickname she called him ever since childhood.

Again, there was no response. She turned the doorknob and opened the door and walked in. The room reeked of alcohol. She stands there holding the tray of food in her hand and calls out to him again.

"Pappy, here, wake up you need to eat."

Savius jumped up out of his sleep gazing at her with a look of fear on in his eyes as if he had just seen an intruder. He actually thought he had locked his bedroom door before passing out on the bed and going to sleep, that's another reason why he was so startled. He yells out in an aggressive manner.

"Come on Ma, how did you get in here? Stop doing that!"

"You have to eat. You can't stay up in this room and just wither away."

"I'm not hungry. Can you just turn the light back off and close the door? "

"Just have a little bit, that's all I'm asking."

"Ma, come on I said I'm not hungry."

He throws the blanket over his head to block out the bright light that had illuminated the whole room. Ms. Lexi set the tray of food down on the night table and walked out the room. The next morning, she gives Prez a call.

"Hey Denny, it's Ma how you doing?"

She's called Prez Denny ever since he was a young child and he always referred to her as Ma. Prez looked at Ms. Lexi like a 2nd mother. There was times when she would call out to one or both and it seemed as if she was talking to two different people because of their nicknames.

"Hey Ma. I'm good, what' up how are you?"

"It's Pappy; I'm starting to get worried. He stays closed up in his room. He barely eats, and from what I see he's drinking a lot. I made one of his favorite dishes……"

Prez interrupts with an excited tone in his voice.

"You made Pot Roast?"

"Yes, I saved you some don't worry." He goes back to listening mode.

"Okay. So what happened Ma?"

"Well anyway, not only did he refuse to eat the food, he practically shouted at me and in so many words kicked me out his room. The room reeked of alcohol; there were empty liquor bottles on the floor. I know he is going through a lot because of what happened so I tried to not bother him, but I'm getting scared because it's like things are getting worse not better."

"I haven't spoken to him in two days myself. He said he needed a little time to himself so I respected that. Like you said, I expect him to go through his grieving, that's natural, you know I know a lot about these things and you do need time to yourself. I figured it's only been two weeks which is still very soon since everything happened. But from what you're telling me we don't want to lose him to. I'll give him a call or stop by."

"Okay, Denny thanks. I don't know if his phone is on but if not just call the house and I will hand him the phone."

"Okay, Ma. And oh save me some of that pot roast."

"Okay Denny, I love you."

"Love you too."

They finish their conversation and hang up the phone. An hour goes by and Prez calls Savius on his cell phone and he answered.

"Hello."

"Wad up Save?"

"Damn, my head feel like somebody smashed it with a ton of bricks yo."

"Sounds like a hangover."

"Yeah more like my hangover have a hangover."

He wrestles around for a minute reaching under the bed grabbing up a half empty bottle of Hennessey making the last drink from the night before to the first drink he has at the start of his day. This was becoming quite a routine.

"So what's the plan for the day?

"Shit."

"Come check me around the way, come up out the cave for a minute. Get some fresh air."

"I can do that, Get Ma off my heels for a minute. See you in a few hours or so."

"Bring some of that pot roast Ma made."

"Oh she told you about that?" Savius asked with an inquisitive tone.

"Oh no doubt, now get ya shit right and bring the grub. One!"

"Alright one!"

His feet hit the floor; he walks over to the wall, gazing in the mirror at his bloodshot eyes. This would be the first time in days since he's left the house. Steps into the shower, and lathers up. He walks over to the closet pulling out a t-shirt and pair of jeans, nothing in particular. He goes into the kitchen and serves out Prez's portion of food and headed towards the front door.

"Ma, I'm out. Going around the way to check Prez and give him some of your famous pot roast."

She steps out of the living room with so much pep in her step That she looked like she was practically running. She was so excited that he had actually decided to get out of the house, to her this was a sign that change was on the rise. He gets down to the warehouse and he and Prez sit and talk for a while. But the conversation was very light. Savius wasn't really in a big talking mood and Prez didn't want to weigh him down so just his presence was good enough. Later that night instead of Savius going back home to Brooklyn he decided to stay at the apartment in the PJ's. He wanted to avoid Ms. Lexi making a trouble over him, and monitoring his moves.

He sits back, looking thru his phone at some pictures of him and Dana he had stored in his phone. Sadness crept up on him once again. The whole time he was down at the warehouse with Prez, he didn't touch not one drink. But it was something about him being alone, the flashbacks in his head that occurred on that tragic day that would lead him reaching for a bottle of something.

He only half bottle of Hennessy Privilege in his possession and two bottles of Heineken. He sat there throwing back the rest of what he had straight up. Under normal circumstances he was usually one to take his drinks slow and savor it on the rocks but was obvious he wasn't drinking for pleasure. He then lit a blunt smoking a little weed to dull the pain he was feeling inside.

By the time he was finished smoking and drinking his last Heineken down to the suds at the bottom of the bottle he wanted something more. He went outside to try and catch the liquor store, but by the time he got to where he was going they were already closed. He drives over to the west side and stops in at a local bar called the Puke. He walks in with a downcast pace in his step and takes a seat at the bar looking up at the TV screen with a blank stare gazing at the basketball game that was playing. The bartender walks up and catches his attention.

"Save?" With a slight hesitation in her voice.

"Hey what's up? I wasn't sure if that was you at first."

"Hey Chloe what's up? Whatchu doin in here?"

"Ugh Duh! I'm working silly." She responds with a chuckle.

"Oh, that's what's up." He responds with dry dull and uninterested tone.

Chloe knows about what happened with Dana, and she wanted to express her condolences right away but she notice that he wasn't in the best of moods at this point. It was plain to see that he was already drinking before he even got there so she kind of played things by ear. Ever since their high school years, Chloe had a crush on Savius, but she end up dating her high school sweetheart named Cas. She got pregnant by him and moved to Queens where he used to hustle and they had big dreams of making things happen. Cas was a large, his connects were in Peru and his work was strictly international. He held stain and was doing his thing until the day Narc ran up and raided the place and locked him down. The timing was really messed up because he ends up missing out on the birth of their daughter Nevaeh.

Between spending money on lawyers, maintaining the bills, while still trying to keep up with the lifestyle she had become accustomed to having within three years the money started running out. If that wasn't enough, things took a turn for the worse when some dudes ran down in her house wearing clown mask robbing her for just about everything she had left.

Although this turn of event practically left her broke, she was thankful that she and her daughter made it out alive. The only money she had left over was a small stash she kept hidden in the house, and the money she was building in her daughter's bank account. She pulled all the money together, bounced up quick and moved back to Harlem. She got an apartment on 138th Street and started bartending down at the Puke. In the beginning when Cas first got locked up she would make every effort to go and visit him even bringing the baby with her. But as time went on the visits became stretched out far and in between and now nonexistent once she found out that he wasn't the faithful dedicated boyfriend that he pretended to be.

There were so many times that she was approached by females claiming to have been in a relationship with him, one woman claiming to have a child by him and two stripper cousins that claimed to have held a ratchet relationship based on pay for play for almost six months and they had pictures to prove it. These confrontations were not always based on just talking. She had gotten into a few physical altercations and she was just plain sick and tired of it. This put a real strain on the relationship and since he was locked up it was very hard to defend the word on the streets. From this point on all she wanted to do was just concentrate on getting back on her feet and raise her little daughter and deal with all the other crap when he gets out.

"So what can I get you?"

"Give me a double shot of Hennessy Privilege."

"I gotchu."

She walks down to the far end of the bar pointing her fingers through the bottle tops trying to find his drink of choice. There was one bottle left; it was buried way in the back behind the other bottles on the shelf. The bottle has been sitting there so long that it had some visible particles of dust. She grabs up a small white cloth and wipes the bottle free of dust.

"Damn Save, this one must have been here just waiting for you."

He gives a smile. She pours the double shot and hands him the glass. He throws it back leaving a pinch at the bottom of the glass.

"Gimme another one."

She pulls down another glass and sets it right next to his and begins to pour.

"What's the other glass for?" He asked with a curious look on his face.

"Oh that's for me, let's toast."

"Toast to what?"

"Old friends that's all."

They clang the glasses together and throw back their shots. For Savius it was one after another. You can tell he was really getting drunk Chloe notice that Savius was already feeling quite nice from the moment he first took a seat so she figured, hey let him go all out and do his thing. She already planned in her head after the second drink she was not going to let him leave there alone and drive back to Brooklyn or back over to Wagner. Hands down he was going back home with her. She lived within walking distance of the bar; he can leave his car parked and go home in the morning. He almost managed to finish off the bottle of Privilege but Chloe cut off his servings.

"You know you going home with me tonight right?"

"Whatchu mean?"

"Exactly what I just said. You know how they say it. Friends don't let friends drink and drive. I live just a few blocks away, we can catch a cab and you can crash at my place till morning."

She turns on the lights in the bar and announces the last call for alcohol. By this time there are only two other patrons in the bar besides she and Savius. She stacks up the chairs and wipes down the tables and the bar top. After she she is finished washing the glasses and putting them away, she taps Savius and tells him it's time to go. They get outside and she flags down a cab. They arrive at her apartment; luckily she only lives on the first floor, so it was no problem getting him into the apartment. Once they get inside, she pulls out her sofa bed, gets some fresh linen and fixes up the bed. She fluffs out the pillows and helps him to lie down. She takes off his shoes and places the cover over him, turns off all the lights and made her way to her bedroom and called it a night.

The next morning, Savius woke up a little unclear of his surroundings. He looks around for a minute and catches view of a Chloe's little daughter Nevaeh. Neveah is standing holding her doll baby in one hand and a brush in the other. She is looking at Savius with a little smile on her face. He smiles back at her and she runs off into the kitchen where Chloe was preparing a simple breakfast.

"Mommy, your friend is up." She says with a bashful blush on her face.

"Ok, Nevaeh, bring this in there and put it on the table and try not to make too much noise ok?"

"Okay Mommy."

Nevaeh places the plate down on the coffee table. The plate had two slices of toast and scrambled eggs. A moment later Chloe enters the room, with a cup of black coffee and a couple of aspirins and hands it to Savius.

"Good morning sleepy head or maybe I should be saying good afternoon." He smiles while holding his head in his hand.

"Good morning, what's this?"

"It's the remedy to that hangover I'm sure you already have."

He takes the aspirin and frowns hard after chugging down the coffee. He looks up at Nevaeh and she is laughing and pointing at him.

"Mommy why he looking like that?"

"Because he just took medicine, you know the same way you make faces when I give you your medicine when you have a cold or something."

"What's your name pretty girl?"

"My name is Nevaeh. What's yours?"

"My name is Savius."

She starts chuckling while twisting around with a shy type of body language.

"Okay Nevaeh let Savius have his breakfast you can go in the room and color me something pretty. Tell Savius bye-bye."

"Okay, Bye bye." She skips off into the room, while looking back a couple of times at Savius smiling.

Chloe hands Savius the plate of food.

"Here, you need something on your stomach. Try to eat as much as you can before it gets cold."

He starts to eat the food and begins short conversation.

"She is such a little cutie and she seems real bright Chloe."

"Aww, thanks Save. That's my life right there."

He finished eating the breakfast and they sat and talked a few more minutes. He was about to leave and wanted to say bye to Neveah again.

Chloe went into the bedroom to get her. Just as they were both walking back to the living room so she can say goodbye, Savius's phone rings. He looks takes the phone out of his pocket and looks at it and its Ms. Lexi. He answers the phone throwing it on speaker as he is putting on his jacket.

"Hello?"

"Hello Pappy? Are you okay? You didn't come home last night I'm making sure you're okay?"

"Yes Ma, I'm good. I just stayed uptown last night."

"Okay, I'm just checking. See you when you get home."

"Okay Ma, see you in a little while."

"Okay Pappy."

After his brief telephone conversation with his mom he puts his phone back in his pocket. Chloe and Neveah are both standing there looking at him.

"Nevaeh, say bye to Savius."

Nevaeh snickers looking up at her Mom with her arm wrapped around her leg.

"His name is not Savius silly." Laughing.

"His name is Pappy." Savius interjects.

"I have two names. My mother calls me Pappy and everyone else calls me by my real name."

"Can I call you Pappy?"

"Nevaeh." Chloe interrupts with a sound of embarrassment in her voice.

"No it's okay, I think it's cute. Sure you can call me Pappy too."

"So only me and your mommy call you Pappy."

She says while running off into the back room.

"Alright Save get home safe and lighten up on the Henney."

"I gotchu. Good looking out to. Thanks Chloe I owe you one."

"Nah we good Save." She gives him a big hug and he walks out the door.

The following day he gives Chloe a call. He wanted to do something nice for her in return for her looking out for him the night before. Chloe really didn't look at it as doing something big. She was just being a friend but Savius would not take no for an answer. She agreed to let him take her and Nevaeh out to dinner.

"Nevaeh, come let's get dressed. Savius is taking us out to dinner tonight. Let's put on something pretty."

"Are we gonna get in a car?"

"Yes we are going to get in Savius's car, now come let's get ready."

"Yaay! We going to dinner with Pappy."

From the moment Savius laid eyes on the baby his heart melted right away. She had these big pretty brown eyes, head full of curly hair and olive complexion. She had a very bright and bubbly personality and was very smart for a four year old. As time went on Savius would spend a lot of his free time hanging out with Chloe and Nevaeh. This seemed to be the perfect remedy for getting him through his dark days. They would do fun things like take Neveah to the movies, Chuck E Cheese, arts and craft shows, the park etc.… Although they spent a significant amount of time together they never crossed the line of becoming any more than friends. Chloe's relationship with Cas was still up in the air and Savius wasn't ready to get serious with anyone since Dana.

CHAPTER TWENTY-NINE

Six months passed by and Prez and Khandi are now planning their wedding. A lot of time and preparation was put into their big day. Savius would be the best man and Donna would be the Maid of honor. The rest of the wedding party included Kizma, Chloe, Terri, Roof, Raze and Swift. Solomon's girlfriend was due to have her baby the same week as the wedding so he couldn't afford to take the chance of being out of town.

Months raced by and it's now a week before the wedding. Prez and Khandi planned the wedding party dinner at their house. Savius was not exactly excited about seeing Donna for the first time since Dana had passed away. He and Chloe were talking one day and the topic came up.

"Chloe man, I don't know how I'm gonna react when I see Donna since everything that has happened."

"Well you know Save, you and Donna have always been close. I'm not trying to defend her or take sides or anything but in spite of her tactics she meant well. You know she's always been the protective type, but it's her delivery that gets things all fucked up."

"Yeah that's true, but you know I still have a sore spot."

"I can only imagine how you feel, but honestly Save she may have done the extreme nosey but that thing that transpired after that really had nothing to do with her. It's better to let it go and move on. I mean things will probably never go back to being the same way between you two but there is no room to hold on to bitterness because you've come so far."

"You right Chloe; I guess it won't hurt if I take it slow and at least holla at her when I see her. What would I do without you?"

Chloe is smiling hard on the other end of the line but she keeps her composure. She is really feeling Savius and they have gotten really close over the months but she continues to keep it strictly platonic so she won't complicate things when Cas comes out.

The day of the wedding party dinner, Savius picks her up and they go together. When Savius walks in the door everyone is sitting around the table laughing and talking and excited to see them both. Donna gets quiet because she is nervous at this point. She sits there biting on her nails and holding on to her wine glass. Savius says hello to everyone including her.

"Hey Dee what's up, how u?"

"Hey Save, I'm good. Just chilling."

She stands up and gives him a quick hug. Donna is so shocked that he actually spoke to her and happy at the same time. She was suddenly able to set her mind at ease and enjoy the rest of the evening. They ate, drank and partied until the early morning.

The following week, Savius planned a Bachelor Party for Prez. Khandi had one request and that was for Prez to be in his own home and wake up in his own bed the morning of the wedding. So Savius decided to have the party start that Thursday and linger into Friday but they would cease all activities by Friday night this way he can honor his wife to be request waking up in his own bed.

Epilogue

The following Thursday Savius rented the Presidential suite at the Waldorf Astoria on Park Avenue. He threw Prez a Bachelor Party. They had plenty of food, drinks, music and different strippers Thursday and Friday it was all in the name of fun.

7:15 AM, Saturday morning the alarm clock goes off playing the tune of Toni Braxton's "Love Should of Brought You Home Last Night", as Prez reaches over and pounds the snooze button for the 3rd time, he is now feeling the aftermath of the Bachelor party Savius threw for him the night before. The night that Prez refers to as "The Prezidential Affair". Savius enters the mahogany room, Prez's bedroom, with a cup of piping hot coffee in one hand and two aspirins in the other shouting from what seemed like outer space at the time.

"Rise and shine homey today's your big day, you get laced forever with that Ole ball and chain.", as he laughs out loud. Prez doesn't utter a word he lays there in his king size dark mahogany sleigh bed wrapped tightly in his black satin Pierre Cardin sheets.

Savius places the coffee and aspirin on the mahogany cocktail table and motions over to the window, draws back the black sheer Valentina curtains pulls up the cranberry roman blinds exposing the sun as it beams straight thru the window. Prez grabs his goose down quilted pillow with satin finish and throws it over his face after telling Savius he thinks he's going to be sick.

DUET

"Yo Prez man its 7:25 and you don't have much time to get your shit together, the limo will be here in less than two hours and we still have to pick the rest of them niggas up, you know how Khandi is real big on time and she'll thrash both our asses if she thinks we slighted her the least bit on her big day, besides you know she will be looking for any reason to get at you because she wasn't feeling the whole B party (Bachelor party) shit anyway."

Savius steps up within breathing space of Prez "So drink this liquid crack." (Black coffee with about 10 teaspoons of sugar) "Swallow this shit; get ya feet wet and lets bounce." Prez pushes up slowly, painfully lifting his head trying to tolerate the internal drum beating in his head.

"Yo Save this shit taste like poison whatcha tryna do kill ya boy?" He and Savius both laughed. Prez steps down off the bed and his feet slowly sink into the black brandy Wilton rug as he makes his way across the room. He slides back the stained glass doors and enters the deep Mahogany finish walk in shower unit. Savius begins to dress for the occasion while at the same time holding conversation with Prez from the other side of the door.

"Yo Prez man I can't believe you and Khandi are finally gonna do this. Y'all 2 been together seems like forever thru thick and thin, right and wrong y'all hold each other down I got mad love and respect for y'all, my blessings always."

With a chuckle in his voice he says "When I grow up I wanna be just like you."

"Thanks man that means a lot." Prez says with a serious tone in his voice.

"Was sup with you and Chloe? I thought you were big on her you know everybody be callin her Wifey and shit."

"All good yo but listen I'm taking shit day by day, she alright and we do what we do, but I think she still a little sweet on her baby daddy, I'll see what it is when homey get out ya heard?"

"That's wassup Save man you doing it right, you gotta hold ya heart in place and pump at your own pace because if you don't bitches out here will try to creep on ya and rip it straight from ya chest. Especially after the shit went down between you and Dana, God Bless, take it easy do what ya do."

"Yo Son finish getting ready let me hit these niggas up and see if they on point."

Savius says with an uneven pitch in his voice. Prez reaches out and grabs the maroon colored Guess towel feeling his way thru as he exits the vapor filled room. He walks over to the armoire takes out a pair of black Bill Blass dress socks, t-shirt and silk boxers, lotions his body from head to toe, sits down on the Chippendale style bench and begins to get dressed.

Prez steals a glance at the easel holding the hand painting of his deceased adoptive parents Mr. and Mrs. Valentine.

"Damn I wish y'all was here right now you'd have something to be proud of in spite of all the messed up shit I've done in my lifetime since y'all been gone." The doorbell rings and it's the limo driver.

"Yo Prez that's us son the whip is here. " Prez dabs on his Gucci envy cologne takes a deep breath and quick glance in the oval shape swing mirror and heads out the front door.

The sun is so bright its glistening off the stretch Lincoln Navigator parked outside.

"Yo Prez you da man this is the type of shit I'm talkin bout." Save is in full spin checking out his whole attire thru the smoked glass tinted windows making sure his shit is tight.

"First Class for you Bro no other way to do it." Prez is standing in front of the house with a baffled look on his face. Patting his pants pockets, sliding his hands thru his double breasted Bill Blass suit jacket reaching into the small satin textured hidden pocket and pulls out nothing.

"Yo Prez waddup? Looking for this? Savius pulls out the wedding ring hoping to take the edge off things.

"I don't know Yo I just have this nutty feeling."

"I gotcha back it's all good, I think you might be getting that nervous jitter type shit that people be talking about."

"Na dog that's for suckers, bitches and shook up muh- fuckers who too stressed to handle their own let's be out Phil Donahue."

"Yo I'm a call the rest of them links and tell them to roll up on the pave since we hard pressed on time."

They pass thru the streets of Harlem sipping on some Dom Perignon White pumping "Meet Me at the Alter by Jagged Edge"; they stop on 122nd Street and 1st Avenue, Wagner Projects, to pick up Swift and Raze. Then precede uptown 138th Street to pick up Solomon and Roof. Without delay they are finally on the way to the church.

They arrive on W.134th Street and the limo comes to a full stop in front of, of Shiloh Baptist Church. The guys enter thru the side of the building. The wedding coordinator is preparing for the ceremony putting the finishing touches on things. Khandi is in the upper room with Kizma, Chloe, Donna and Terri. The girls are dressed in their Champagne colored Donna Karan dresses, shoes and all Donna Karan accessories. Khandi is wearing a beautiful beaded Ivory, colored gown designed by Donna Karan, needless to say that Donna and Khandi's best friend had influence on picking the designer. Khandi's grandmother, Ms. Anne, is with the girls making sure everything goes smooth and she also wants to sneak in a few pictures of her own.

"Ladies gather together because I want to take a few amateur pictures before the photographer comes in."

The girls pose naturally and they take at least ten picturcs before the photographer steps in with his professional detail

"Donna these shoes are fierce and so is the train on this dress, I didn't realize it was so long. You know I'm gonna need your help so I won't fall flat on my face."

"Don't worry girl I got you."

"Oh yeah, gotta follow tradition this is for you, here's your something new."

Donna digs in her bag and pulls out a diamond necklace. Chloe rapidly makes her way over to Khandi holding a blue lace garter belt.

"And here's your something blue."

Terri hands Khandi a little box engraved from Tiffany's, Khandi has a surprised look on her face.

"Girlfriend don't look too surprised I love you and all, but here is your something borrowed."

Khandi opens the box and it's a pair of infinity swirl diamond earrings.

"This has been in the family for a minute, from my great granny, to granny and my moms and me."

"I'll see your ass right after you say I do, Sykes you know I love you girl!"

Kizma pulls out a picture that the group had taken in their freshman year of High School, "And here's something old for ya old ass bitches."

They all begin to laugh, Ms. Annie walks over, "So you have something old, something new, something borrowed something blue well here's my love." she gives Khandi a big hug and whispers in her ear.

"I have something very important to give you later."

The wedding coordinator enters the room.

"Ladies five minutes to Showtime, and by the way you all look beautiful."

The organist begins playing the Brazilian Wedding March. The Wedding party March down the aisle and they are all positioned at the altar awaiting Khandi's arrival. The melody stops and the Organist strike a musical tone as a gesture for the guest to stand.

Khandi makes her entrance. Faint whispers from the mass are heard as Khandi saunters the Aisle with her father, Mr. Kashmen ushering her every pace. Initially she had no intentions of even inviting him to the wedding and above all not having him give her away on her special day. She developed resentment for him resulting from him walking out of her life when she was only eight years old. He walked got dressed one day said he was going to the store, promised to bring back her favorite chocolate flavored ice-cream on a sugar cone and never returned. Since then she detested chocolate ice cream, sugar cones and any constructive thoughts of him. He made contact with her eight years later, the day of her mother's funeral. She shared an emotional detachment for him; especially when she learned that he had re-married and went on to have two other children. Prez was a big influence on her final thought when she decided 2 weeks before the wedding to ask him to partake in the Ceremony.

Reverend Tucker requested that everyone bow their heads in Unison for payer. While the Reverend was leading prayer "Rome, (Mateo's) brother unnoticeably gains access thru the entrance hall and helps himself to a seat near the front of the church. Lisa (Khandi's cousin) glances over and detects him. She instantly has a very uneasy feeling about him being there. Lisa knows that almost a year ago Mateo and Prez had a disturbing confrontation that had a much unexpected result and things got really ugly. With this in mind she knew there was no way that Prez and Khandi would have him on the guest list. Within the few seconds she noticed him, she knew disaster was about to strike. Prayer was over, everyone is seated and Rome has merged in with the rest. Lisa's thoughts are running thru her mind 100 miles a second as she stares over at Rome trying to peep his next move. Khandi declares her vows, finishes her "I Do's" now Prez is proclaiming his vows.

Everything is evolving at such high velocity while Lisa is contemplating a way to signal that something unorthodox is about to go down. Just as Prez is about to declare his "I Do's" preparing to seal it with a kiss, Lisa sees Rome pull out a gun aiming it directly at Prez.

She screams out "Prez!!", but she was seconds too late, shots rang out and Prez is hit.

Author Dez Sabree (BIO)

Dez was born and raised in Brooklyn New York. She graduated Jane Adams High School in the Bronx in 1986. Shortly after she gave birth to her daughter Giovanni and they later moved to New Jersey. Dez became a mother of two after the birth of her son Richard. Dez has always been a dedicated mother and family orientated person. She is now the proud Grandmother of her Granddaughter Brooklynn.. Dez loves to laugh, and has a sense of humor that only those close to her has the pleasure of knowing. She is outgoing yet reserved and a free spirited individual. Dez has a love for life and building a more solid -relationship with God almighty. She currently works in the healthcare industry and in her spare time she loves to write. Writing has always been her passion. Her motto is, born with a pen in her hand and ready to share her work with the world before the ink dries. Dez is the CEO, Founder Mother II Son Publishing LLC. Co-Founded with her Son COO, Richard Sabree-Feimster.

www.ingramcontent.com/pod-product-compliance
Lightning Source LLC
Chambersburg PA
CBHW050401030726
47503CB00006B/1964
9780997798708